MO AND JO
FIGHTING TOGETHER FOREVER

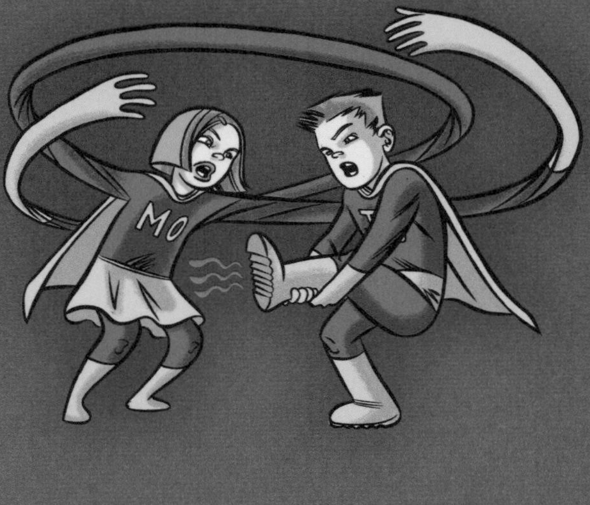
MO

DEAN HASPIEL & JAY LYNCH

MO AND JO
FIGHTING TOGETHER
FOREVER

A TOON BOOK BY

DEAN HASPIEL & JAY LYNCH

THE LITTLE LIT LIBRARY, A DIVISION OF RAW JUNIOR, LLC, NEW YORK

For Mom and Dad

–Dean

For Tristan and Seamus

–Jay

Editorial Director: FRANÇOISE MOULY
Advisor: ART SPIEGELMAN

Book Design: FRANÇOISE MOULY & JONATHAN BENNETT

 Library of Congress Control Number: 2007943850
ISBN 13: 978-0-9799238-5-2 ISBN 10: 0-9799238-5-9

10 9 8 7 6 5 4 3 2 1

www.TOON-BOOKS.com

CHAPTER ONE:

FIGHTING...

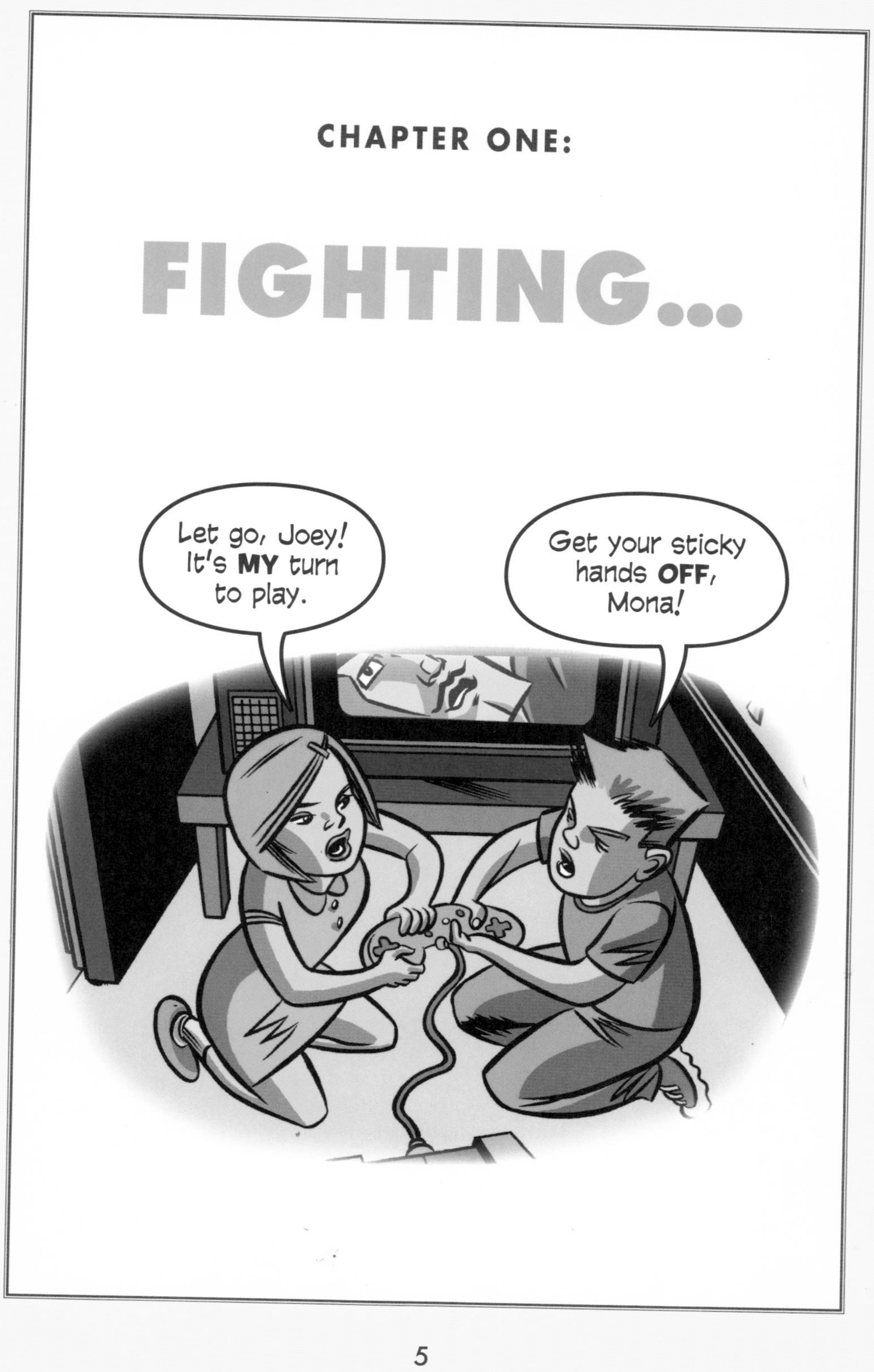
Let go, Joey! It's **MY** turn to play.
Get your sticky hands **OFF**, Mona!

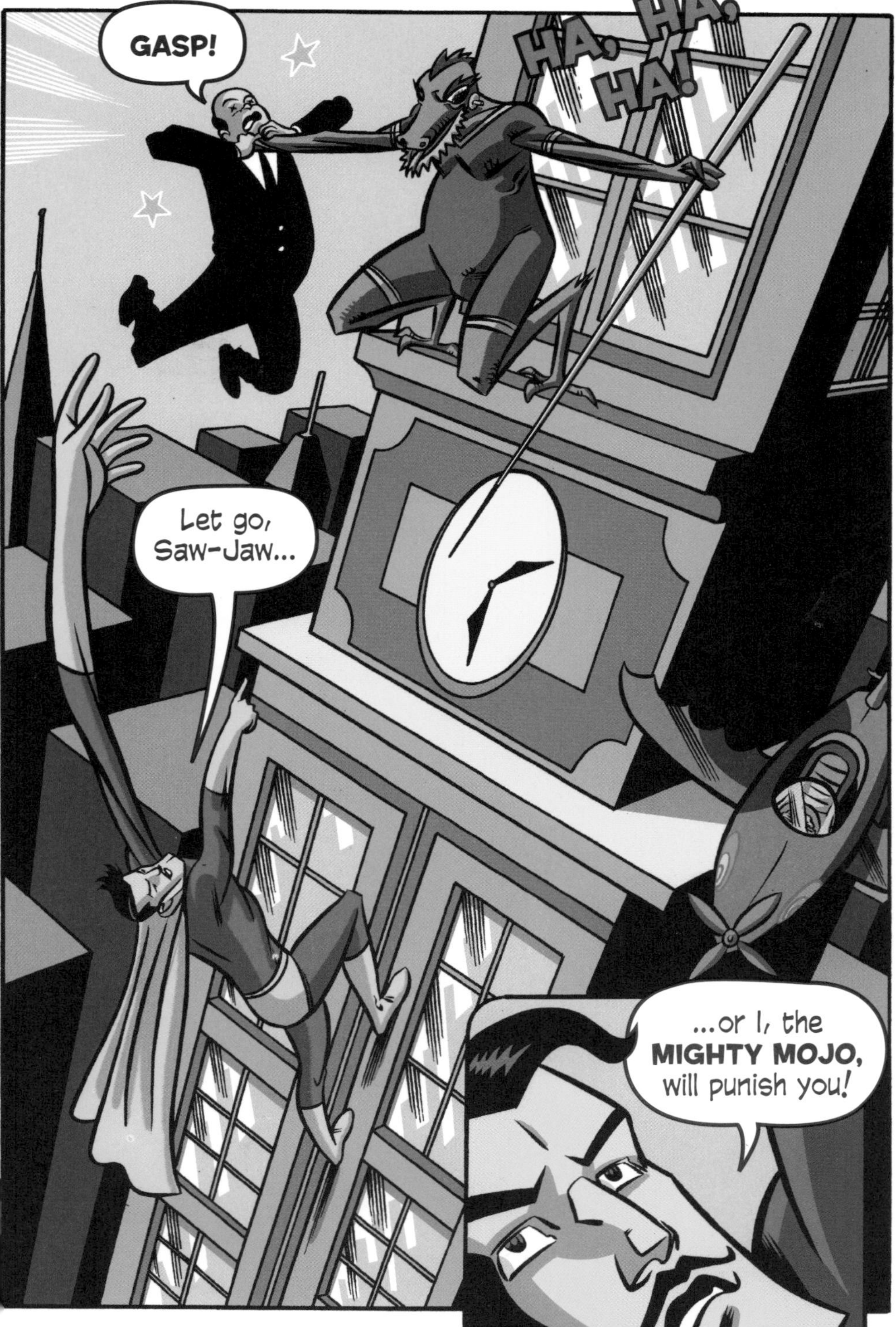
GASP!
HA, HA, HA!
Let go, Saw-Jaw...
...or I, the **MIGHTY MOJO,** will punish you!

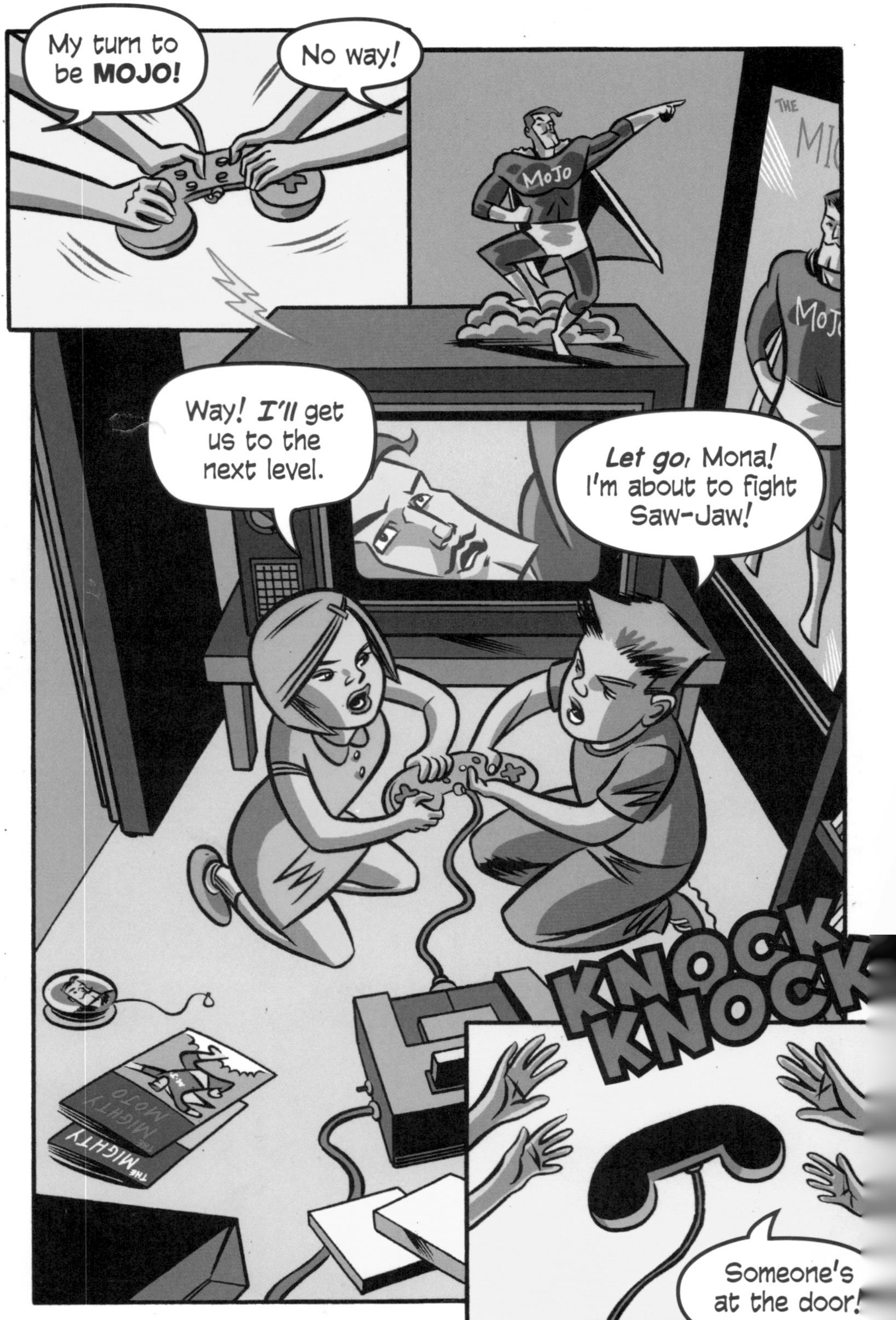
My turn to be MOJO!
No way!
MoJo
THE MIG
MoJo
Way! I'll get us to the next level.
Let go, Mona! I'm about to fight Saw-Jaw!
THE MIGHTY MOJO
THE MIGHTY
KNOCK KNOCK
Someone's at the door!

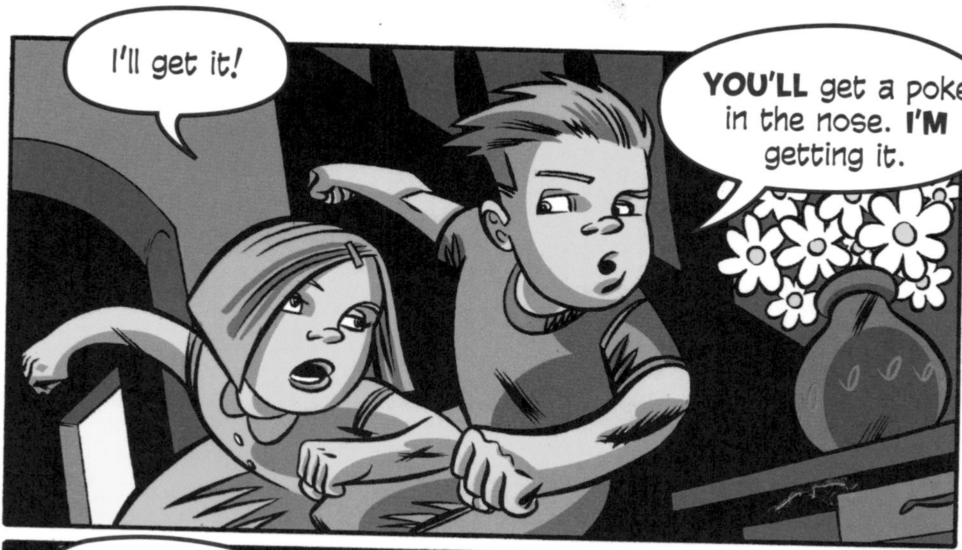
I'll get it!
YOU'LL get a poke in the nose. **I'M** getting it.

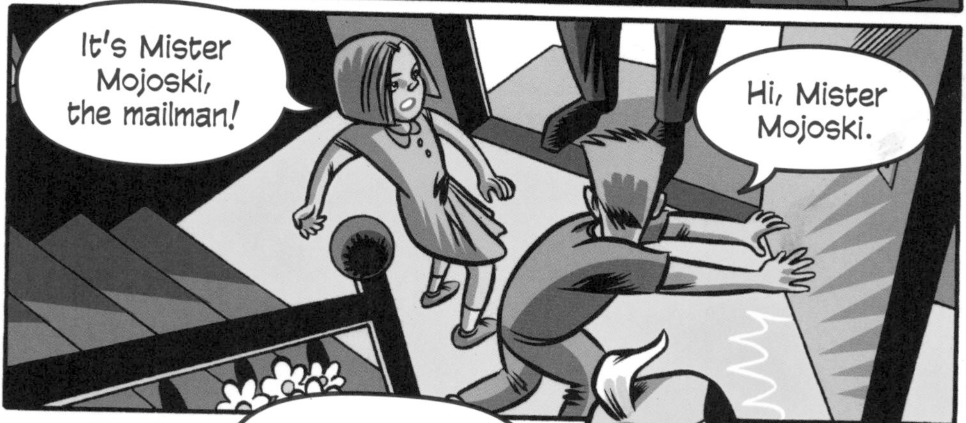
It's Mister Mojoski, the mailman!
Hi, Mister Mojoski.

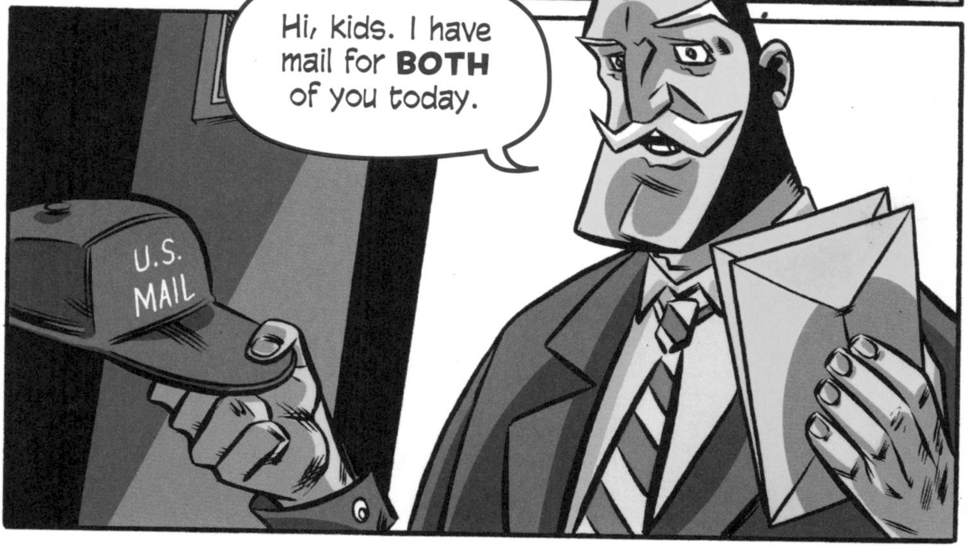
Hi, kids. I have mail for **BOTH** of you today.
U.S. MAIL

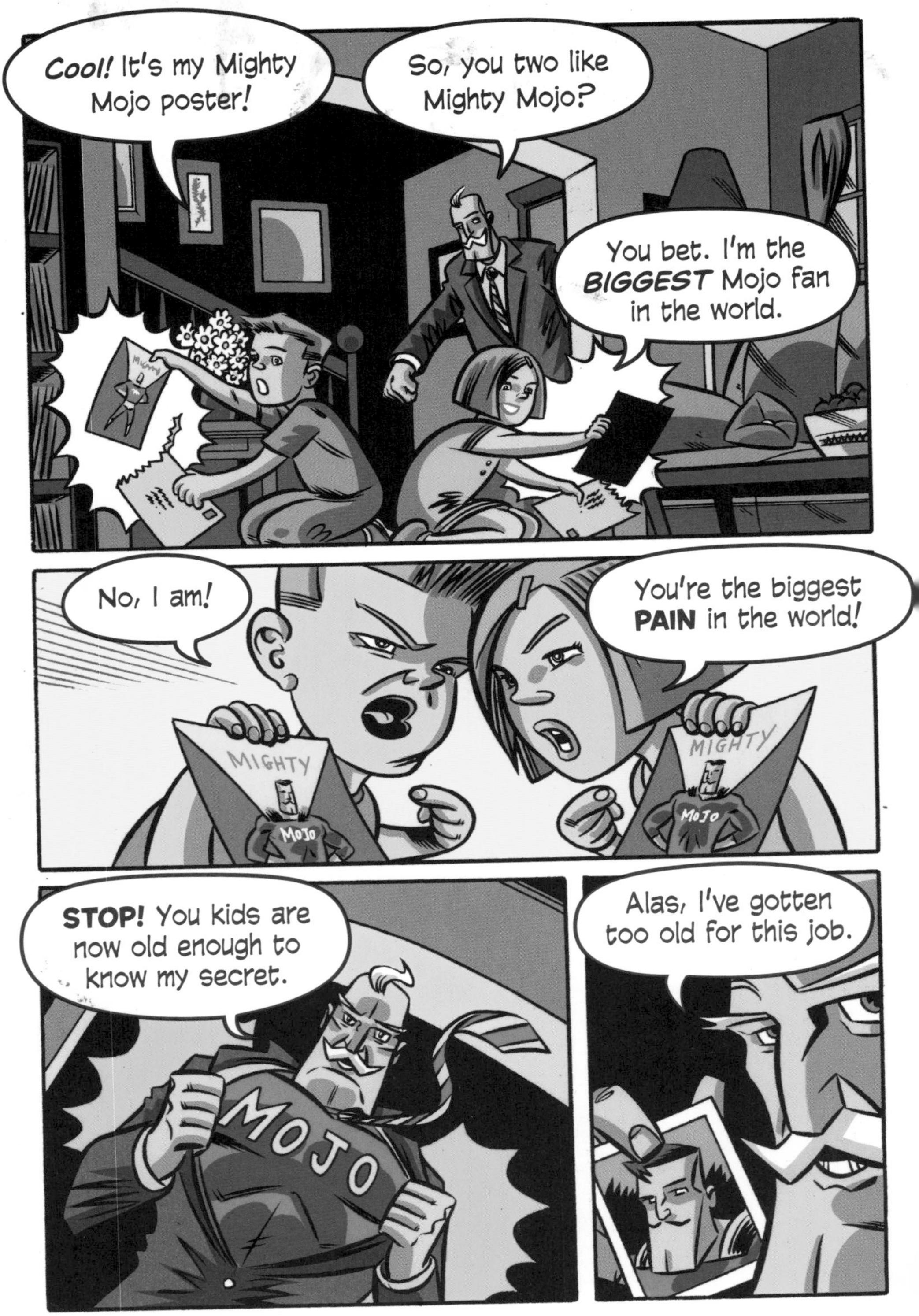
Cool! It's my Mighty Mojo poster!
So, you two like Mighty Mojo?
You bet. I'm the BIGGEST Mojo fan in the world.
MIGHTY
No, I am!
You're the biggest PAIN in the world!
MIGHTY
MOJO
MIGHTY
MOJO
STOP! You kids are now old enough to know my secret.
MOJO
Alas, I've gotten too old for this job.

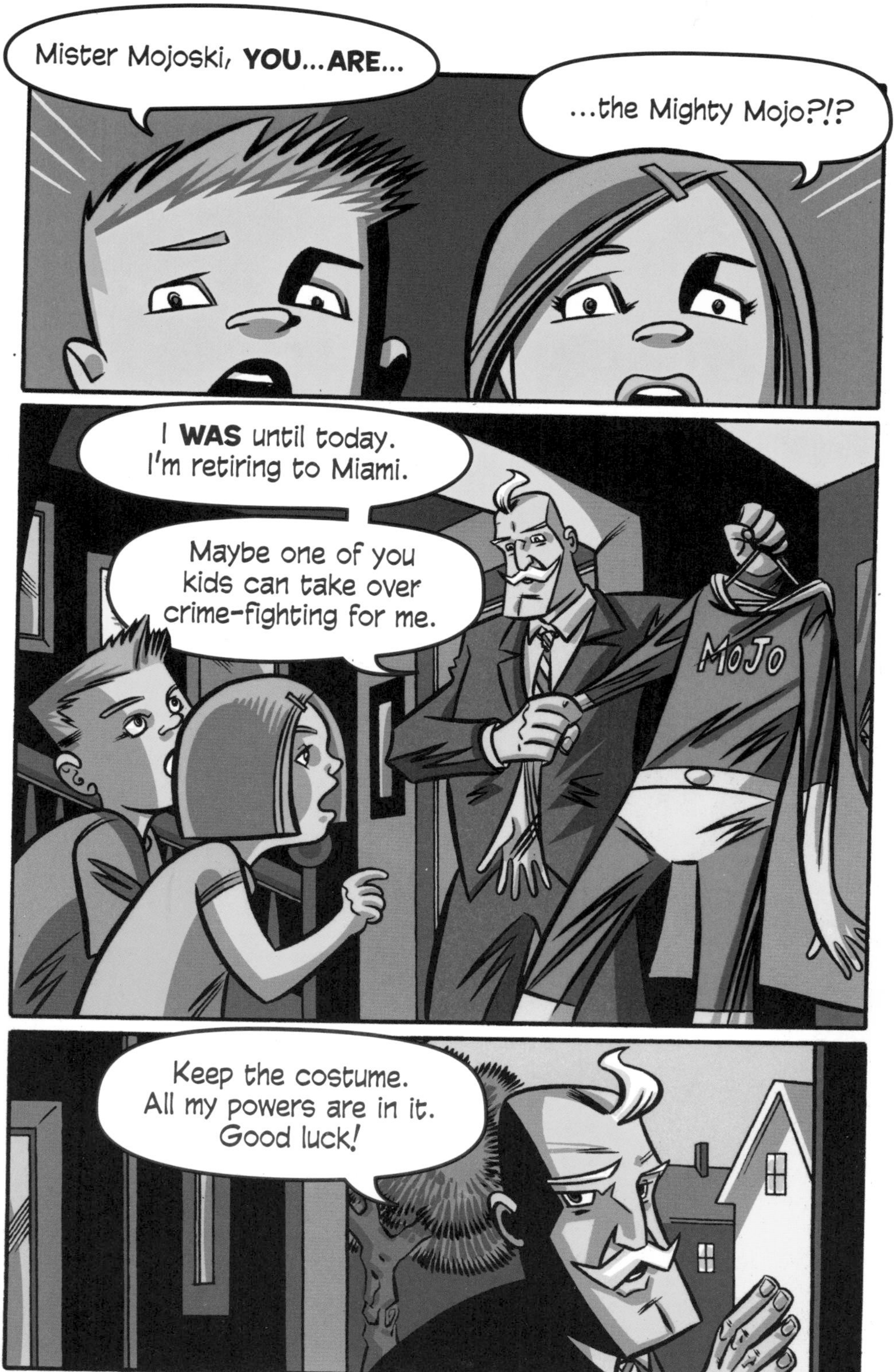
Mister Mojoski, **YOU...ARE...**
...the Mighty Mojo?!?
I **WAS** until today. I'm retiring to Miami.
Maybe one of you kids can take over crime-fighting for me.
MOJO
Keep the costume. All my powers are in it. Good luck!

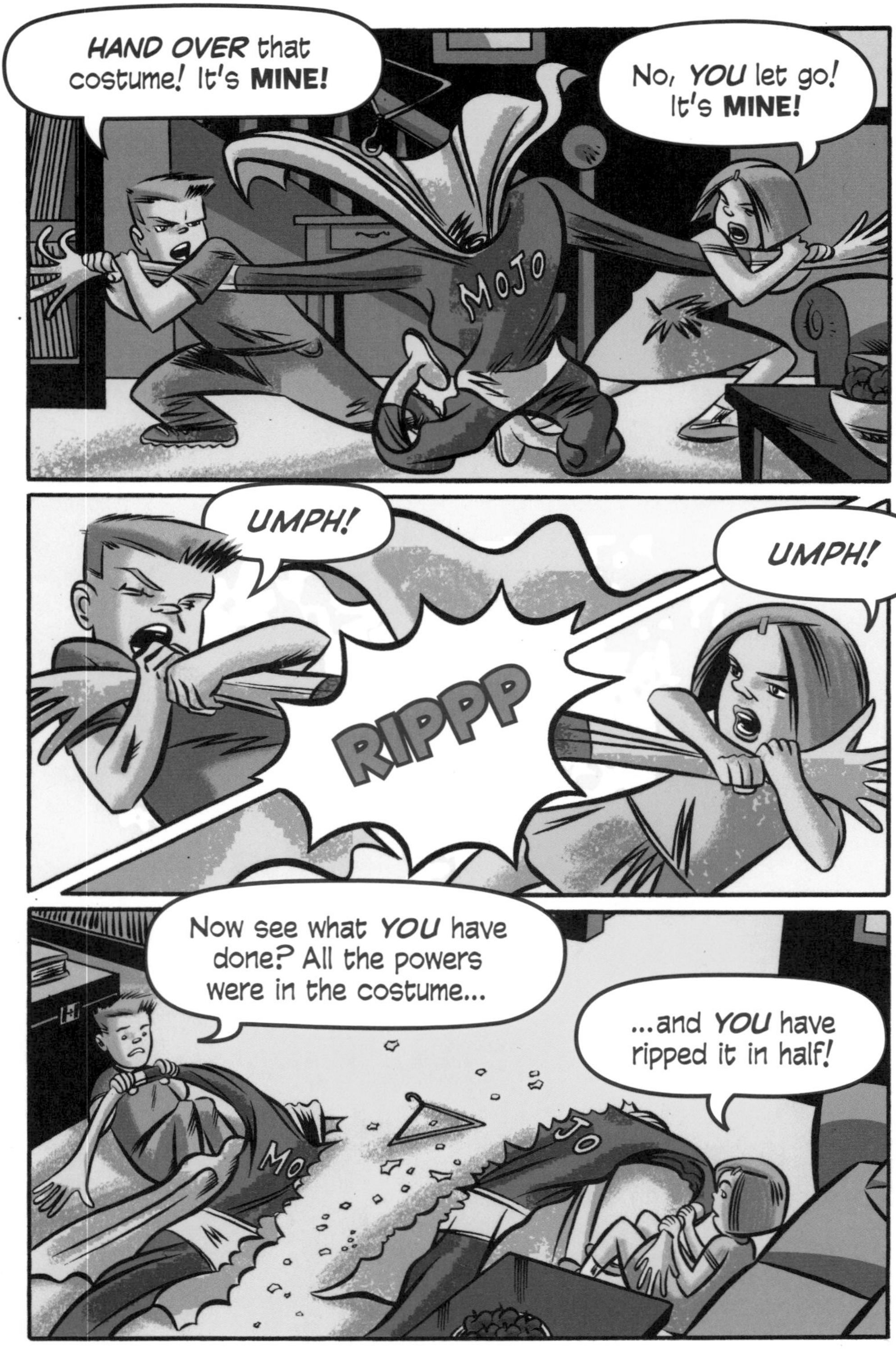
HAND OVER that costume! It's MINE!
No, YOU let go! It's MINE!
MOJO
UMPH!
UMPH!
RIPPP
Now see what YOU have done? All the powers were in the costume...
...and YOU have ripped it in half!
MO
JO

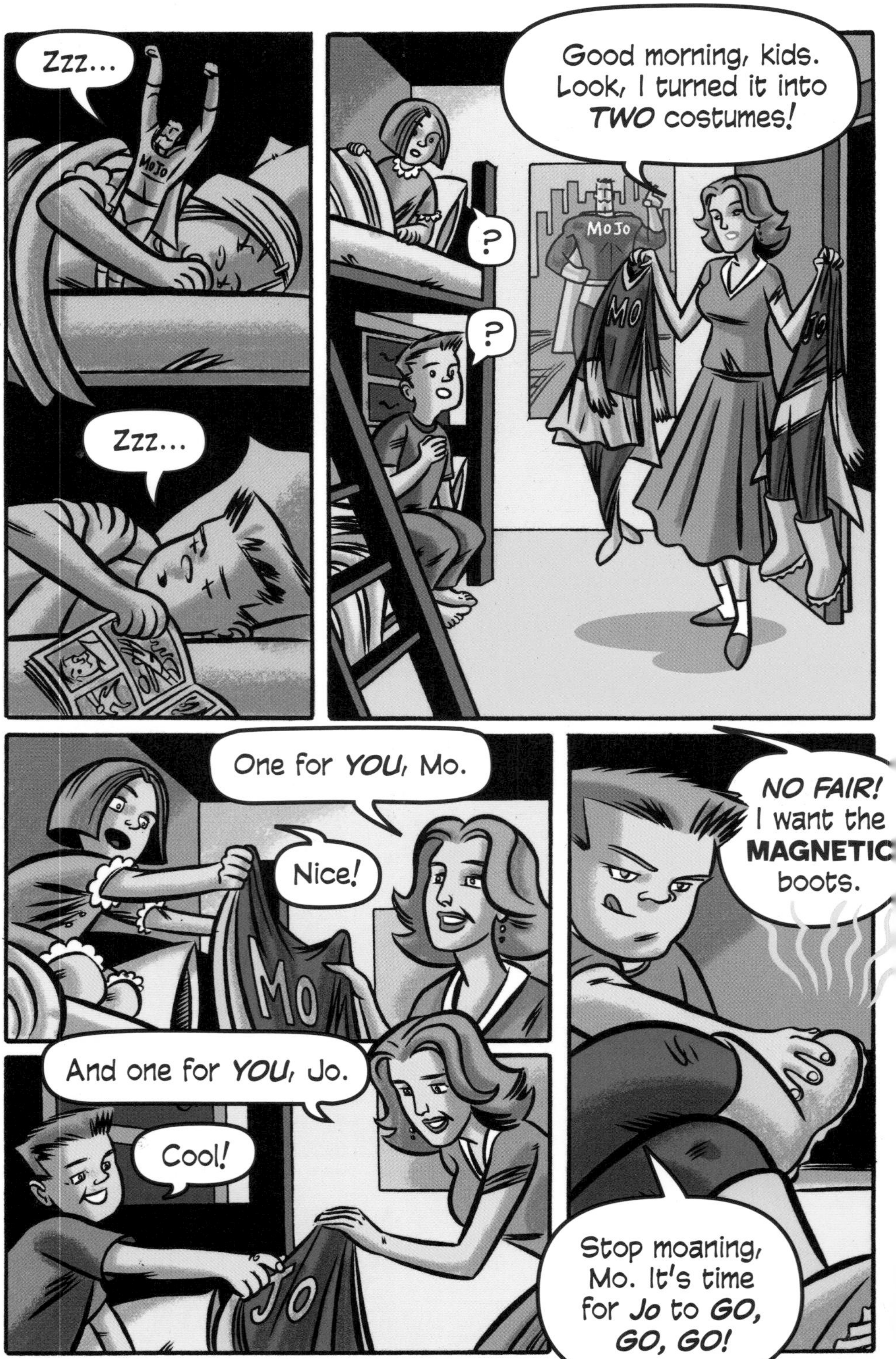
Zzz...
Zzz...
Good morning, kids. Look, I turned it into TWO costumes!
?
?
MO JO
One for YOU, Mo.
Nice!
And one for YOU, Jo.
Cool!
NO FAIR! I want the MAGNETIC boots.
Stop moaning, Mo. It's time for Jo to GO, GO, GO!

CHAPTER TWO:

FIGHTING FOREVER...

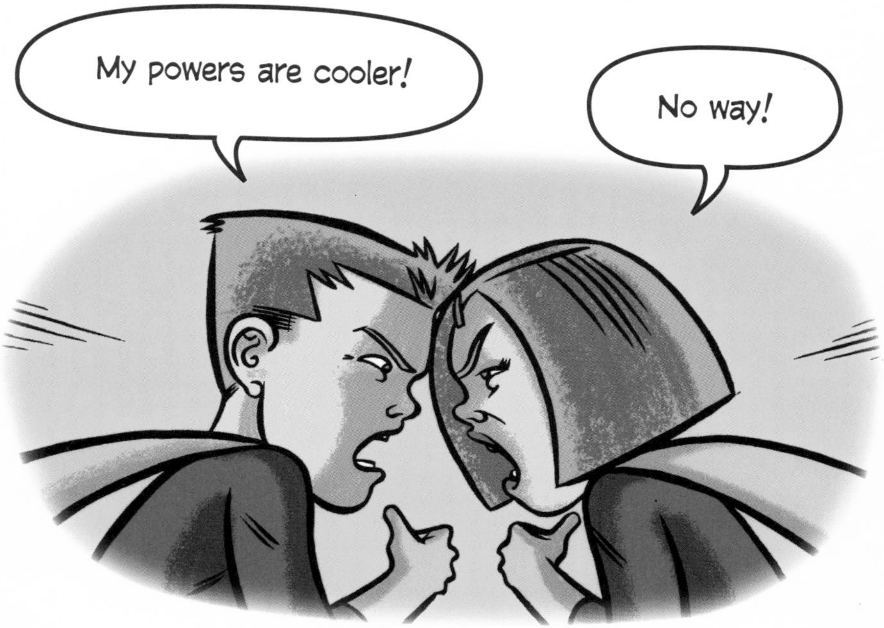
My powers are cooler!
No way!

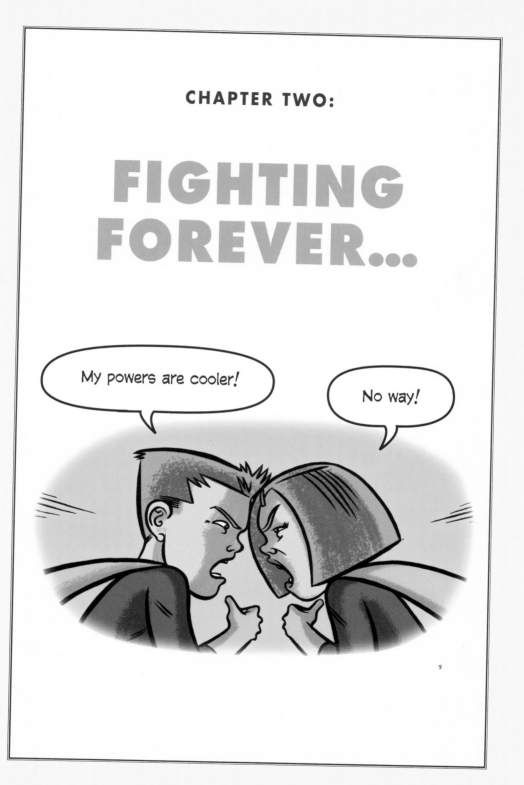

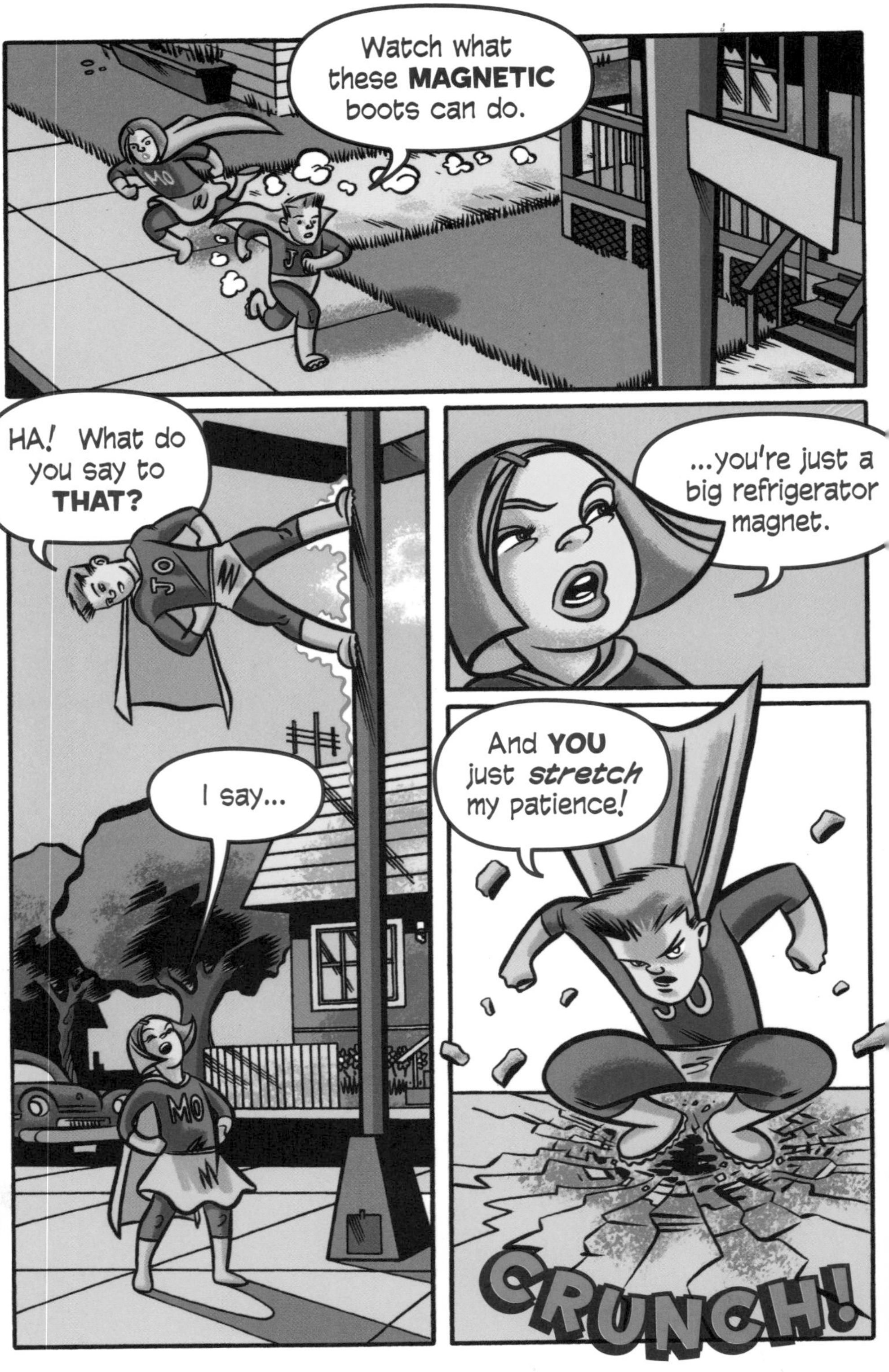
Watch what these MAGNETIC boots can do.
HA! What do you say to THAT?
I say...
...you're just a big refrigerator magnet.
And YOU just stretch my patience!
CRUNCH!

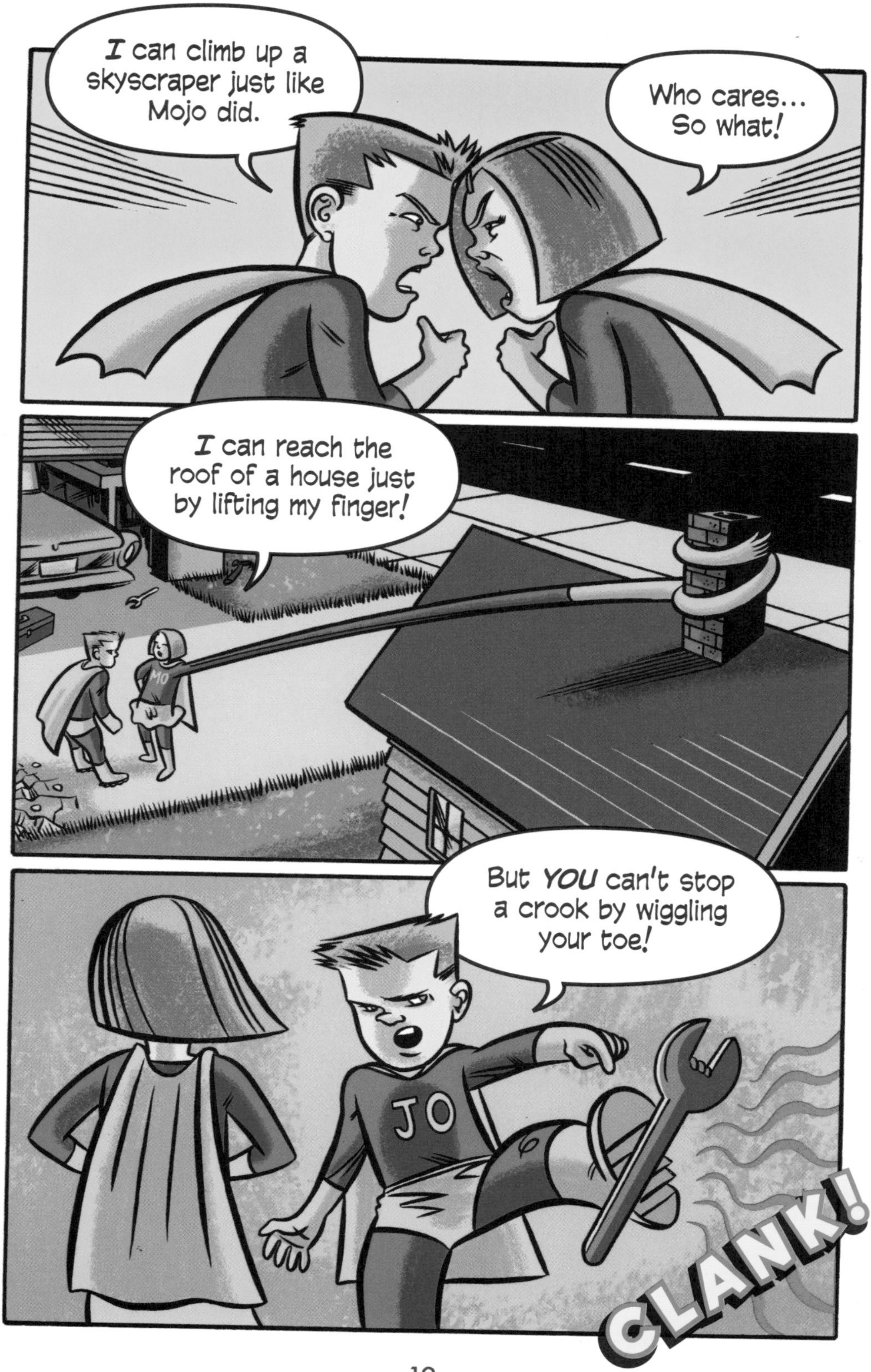
I can climb up a skyscraper just like Mojo did.
Who cares... So what!
I can reach the roof of a house just by lifting my finger!
MO
But YOU can't stop a crook by wiggling your toe!
JO
CLANK!

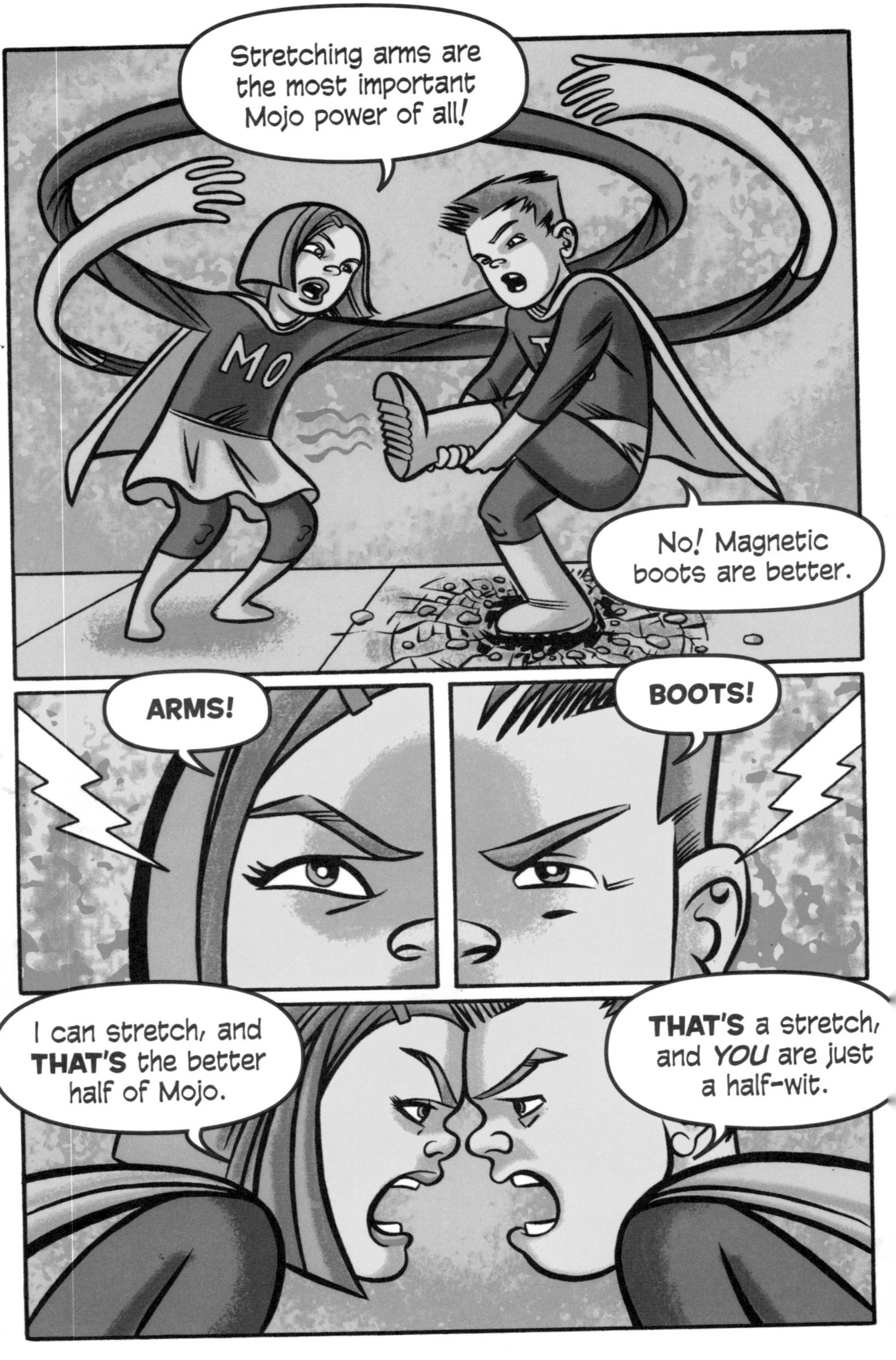
Stretching arms are the most important Mojo power of all!
No! Magnetic boots are better.
ARMS!
BOOTS!
I can stretch, and **THAT'S** the better half of Mojo.
THAT'S a stretch, and *YOU* are just a half-wit.

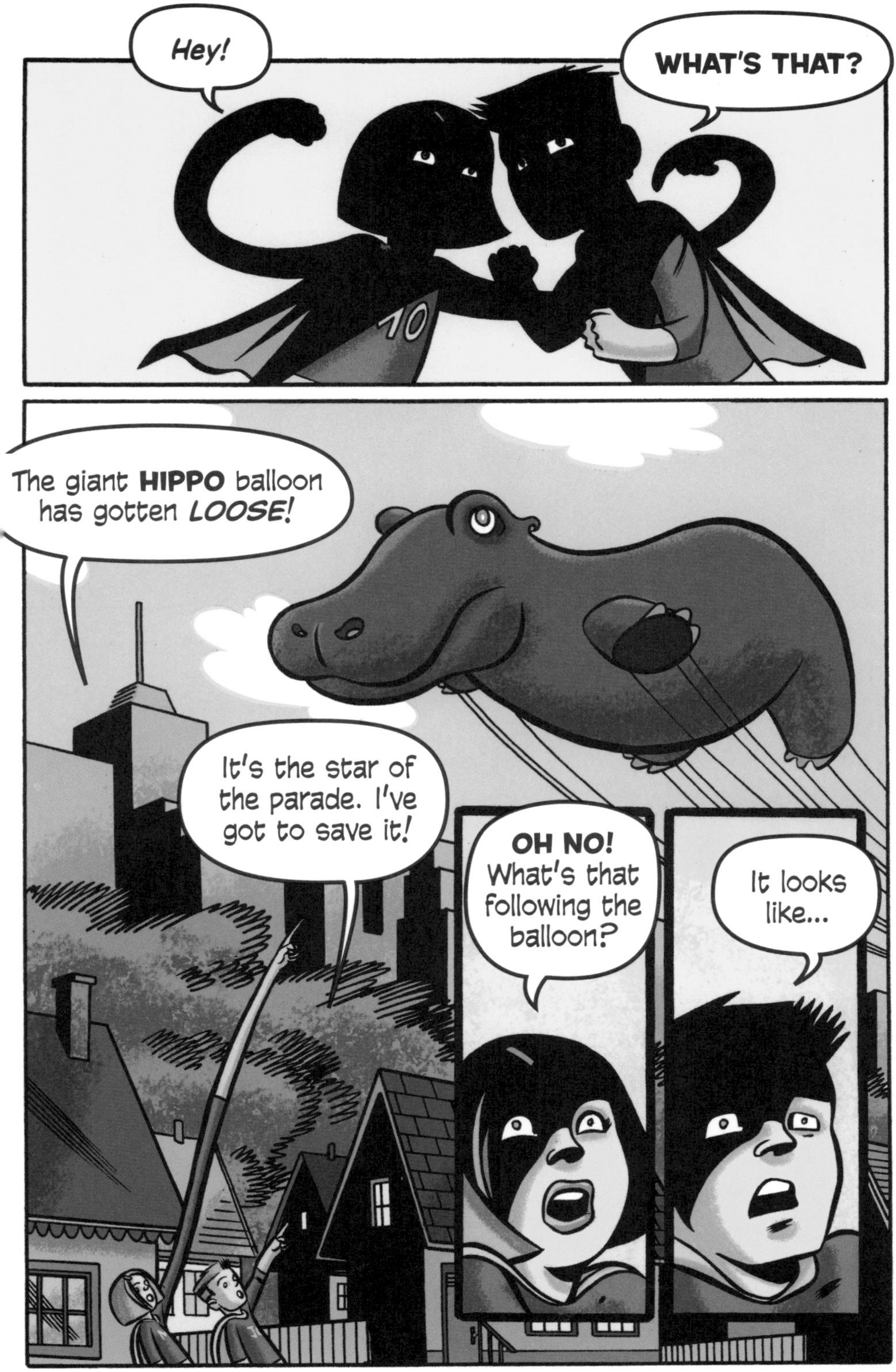
Hey!
WHAT'S THAT?
The giant HIPPO balloon has gotten LOOSE!
It's the star of the parade. I've got to save it!
OH NO! What's that following the balloon?
It looks like...

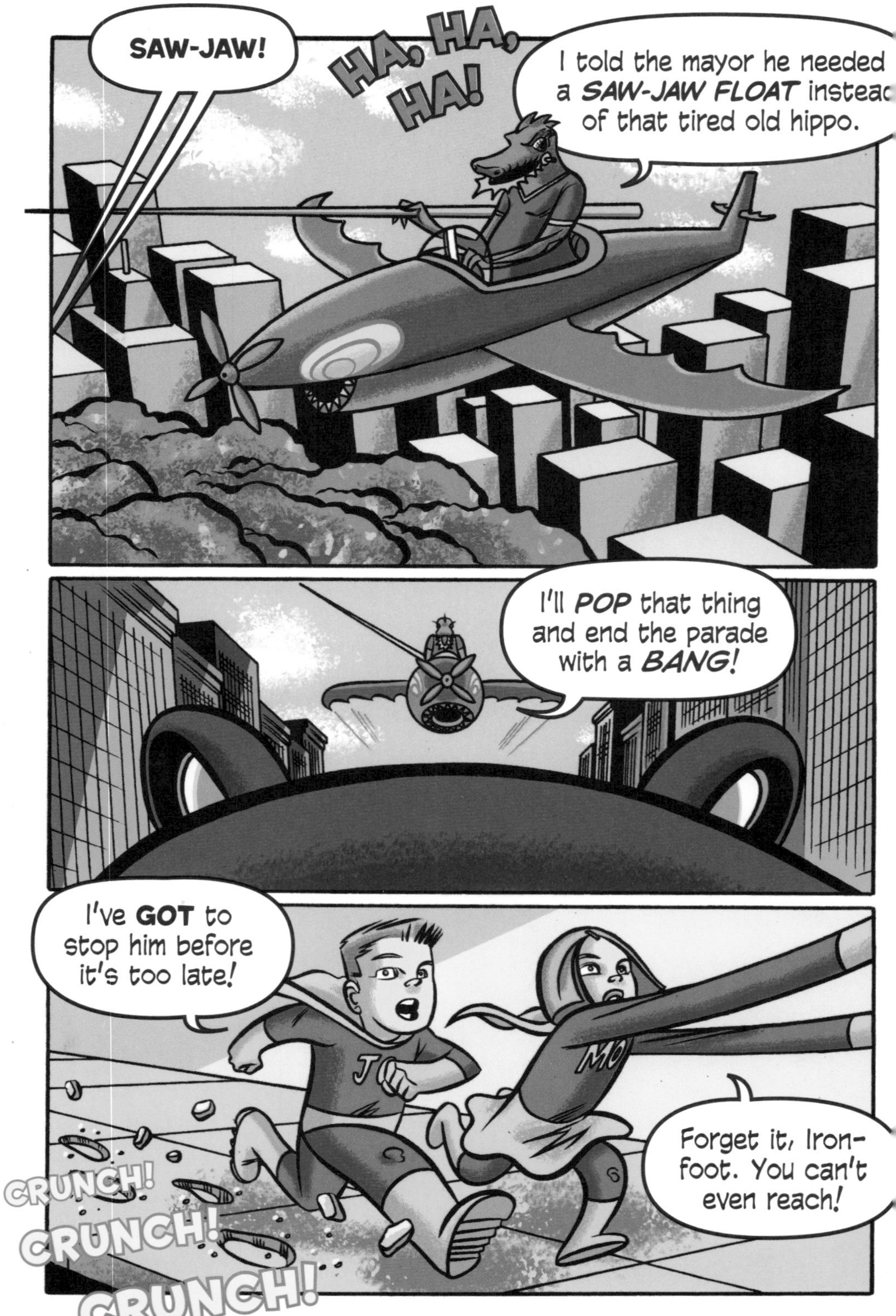
SAW-JAW!
HA, HA, HA!
I told the mayor he needed a SAW-JAW FLOAT instead of that tired old hippo.
I'll POP that thing and end the parade with a BANG!
I've GOT to stop him before it's too late!
Forget it, Iron-foot. You can't even reach!
CRUNCH! CRUNCH! CRUNCH!

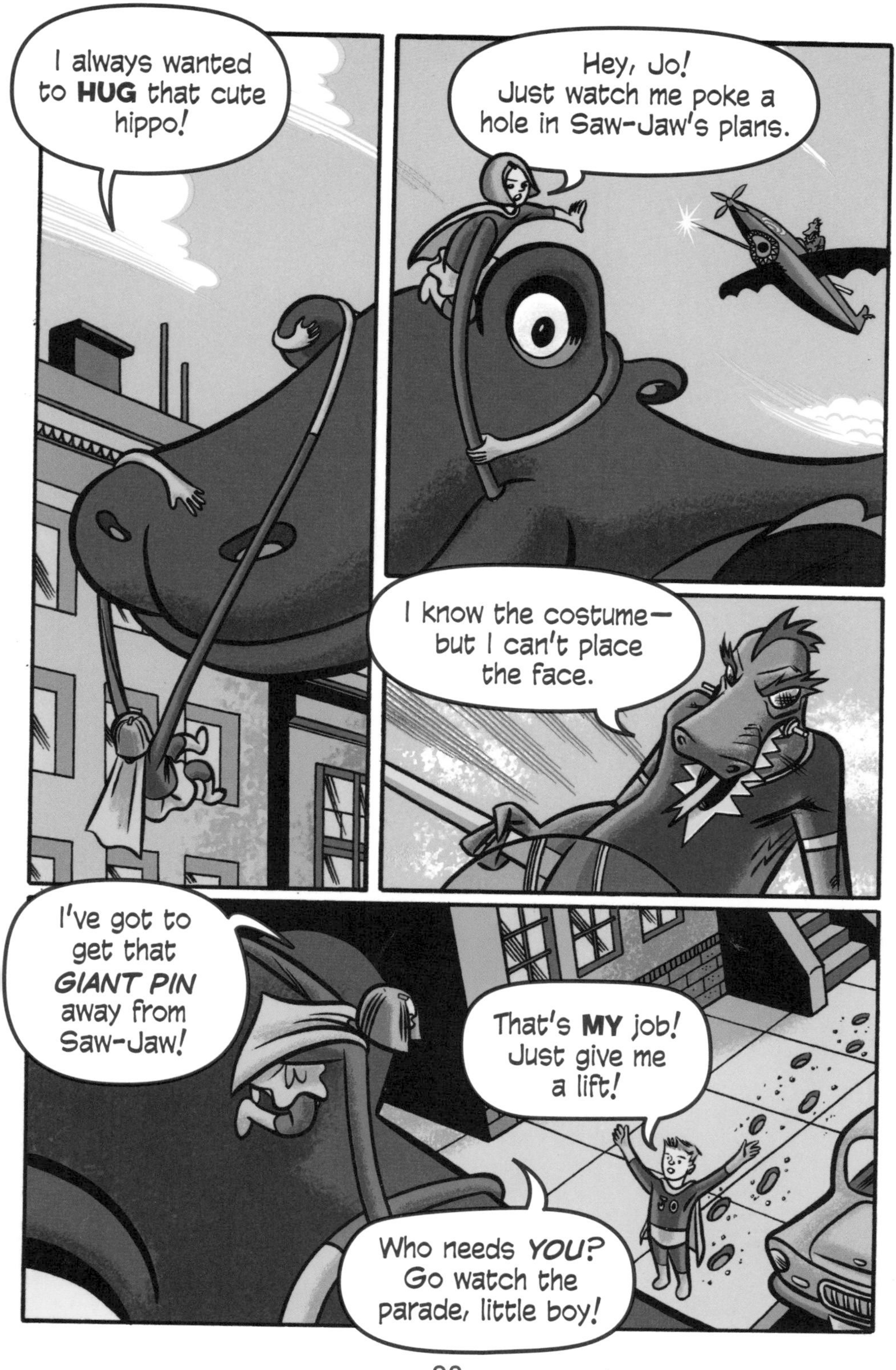
I always wanted to HUG that cute hippo!
Hey, Jo! Just watch me poke a hole in Saw-Jaw's plans.
I know the costume— but I can't place the face.
I've got to get that GIANT PIN away from Saw-Jaw!
That's MY job! Just give me a lift!
Who needs YOU? Go watch the parade, little boy!

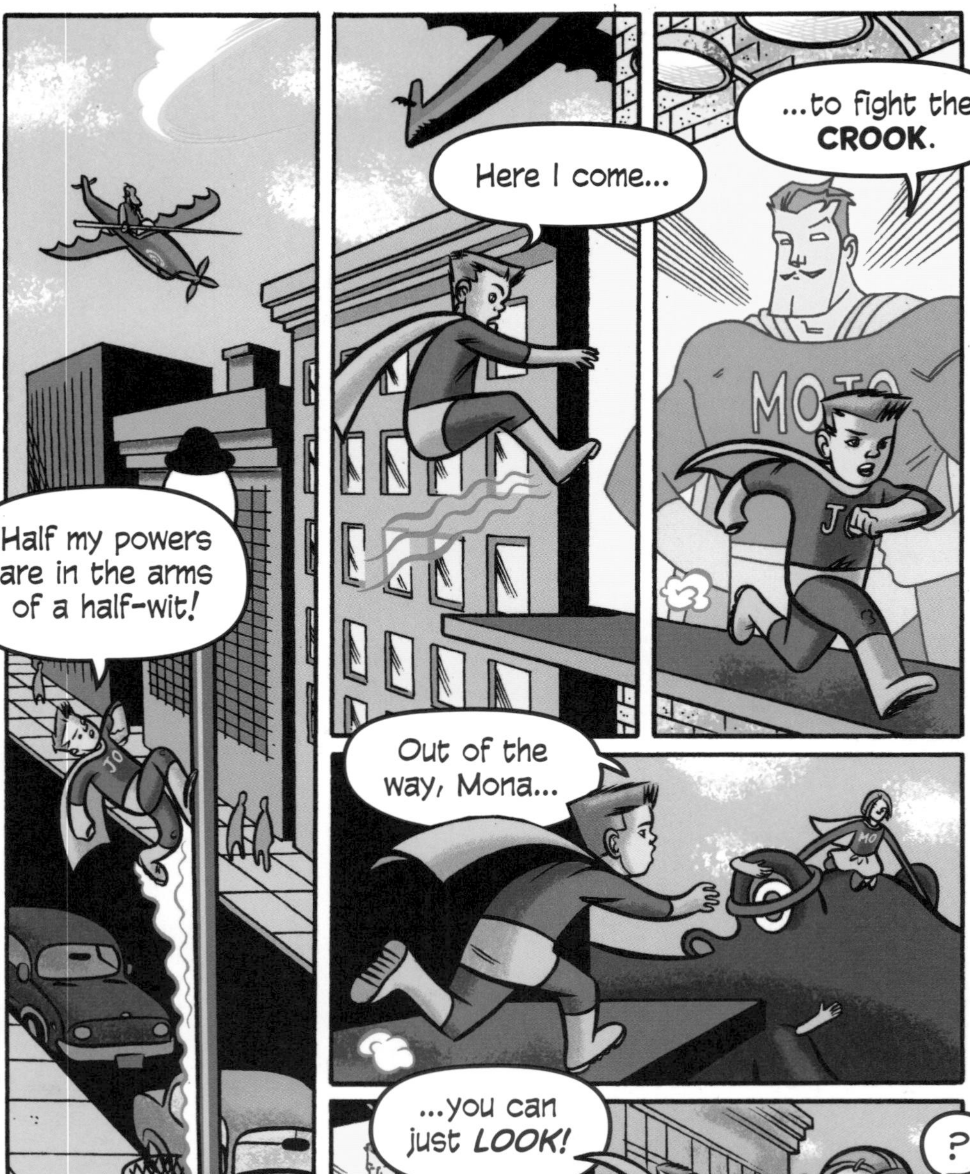
Half my powers are in the arms of a half-wit!
Here I come...
...to fight the CROOK.
Out of the way, Mona...
...you can just LOOK!
?
JO
MOJO
MO

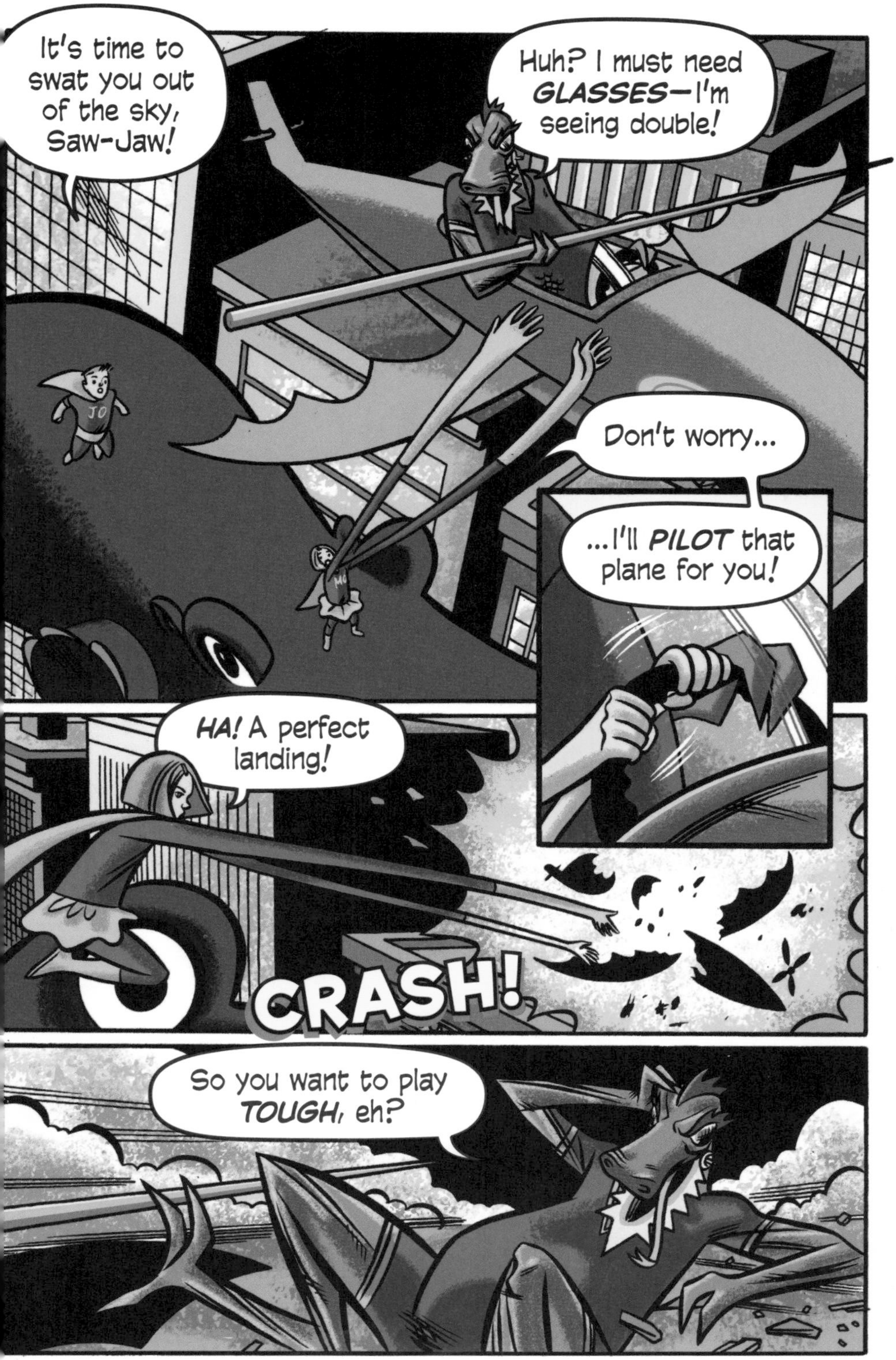
It's time to swat you out of the sky, Saw-Jaw!
Huh? I must need GLASSES—I'm seeing double!
Don't worry...
...I'll PILOT that plane for you!
HA! A perfect landing!
CRASH!
So you want to play TOUGH, eh?

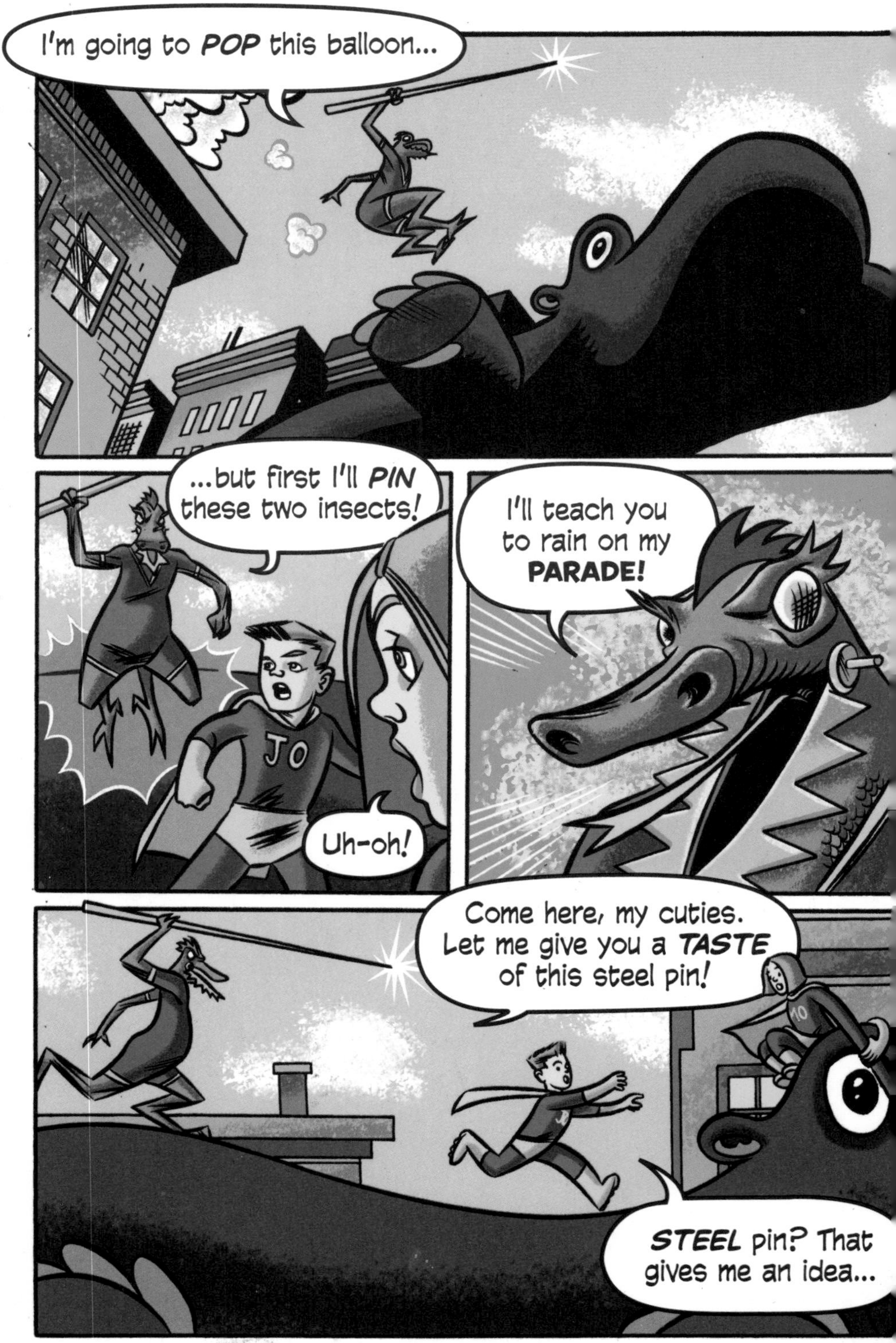
I'm going to *POP* this balloon...
...but first I'll *PIN* these two insects!
Uh-oh!
I'll teach you to rain on my **PARADE!**
Come here, my cuties. Let me give you a *TASTE* of this steel pin!
STEEL pin? That gives me an idea...

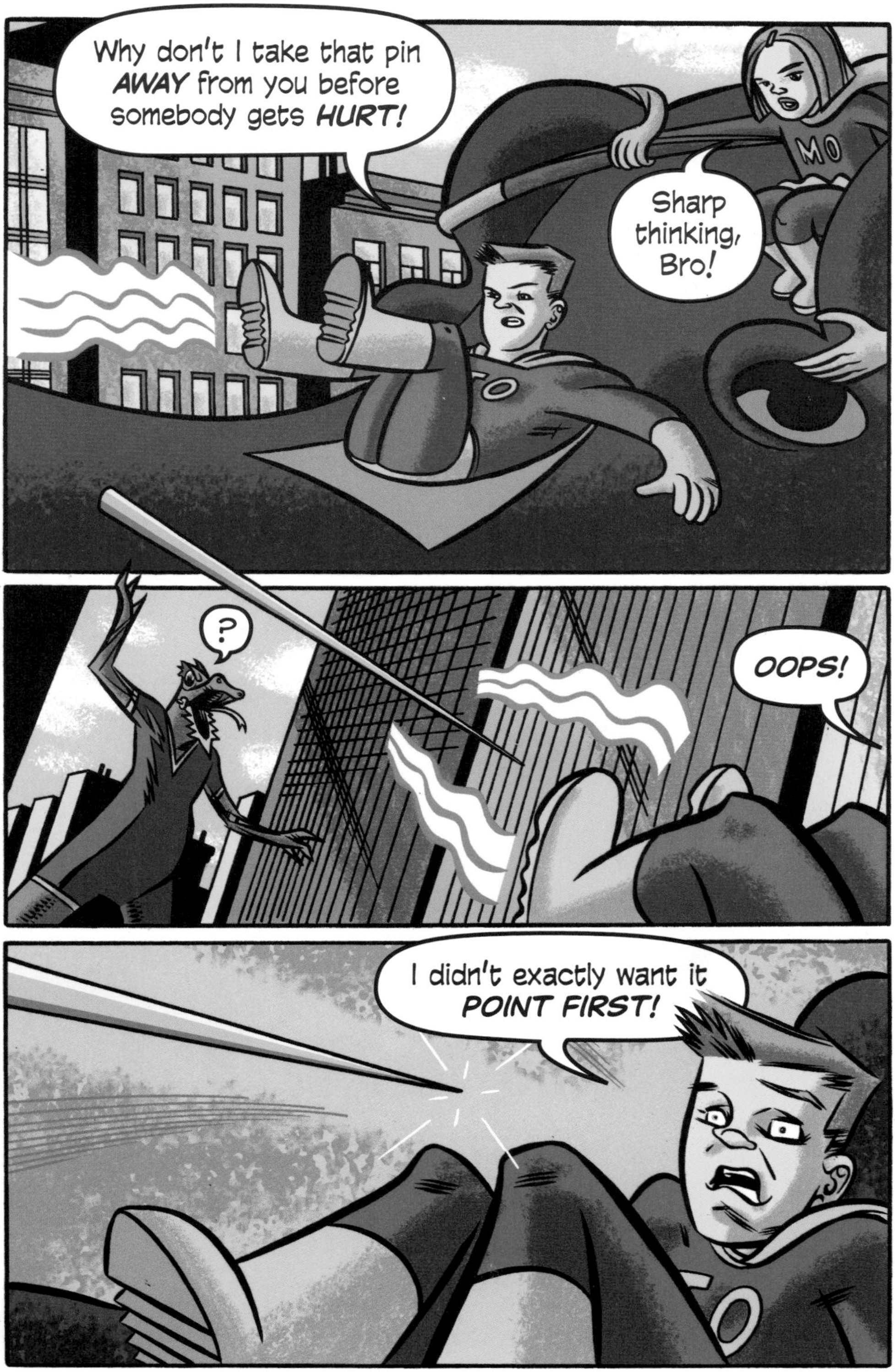

Why don't I take that pin AWAY from you before somebody gets HURT!
Sharp thinking, Bro!
?
OOPS!
I didn't exactly want it POINT FIRST!
MO

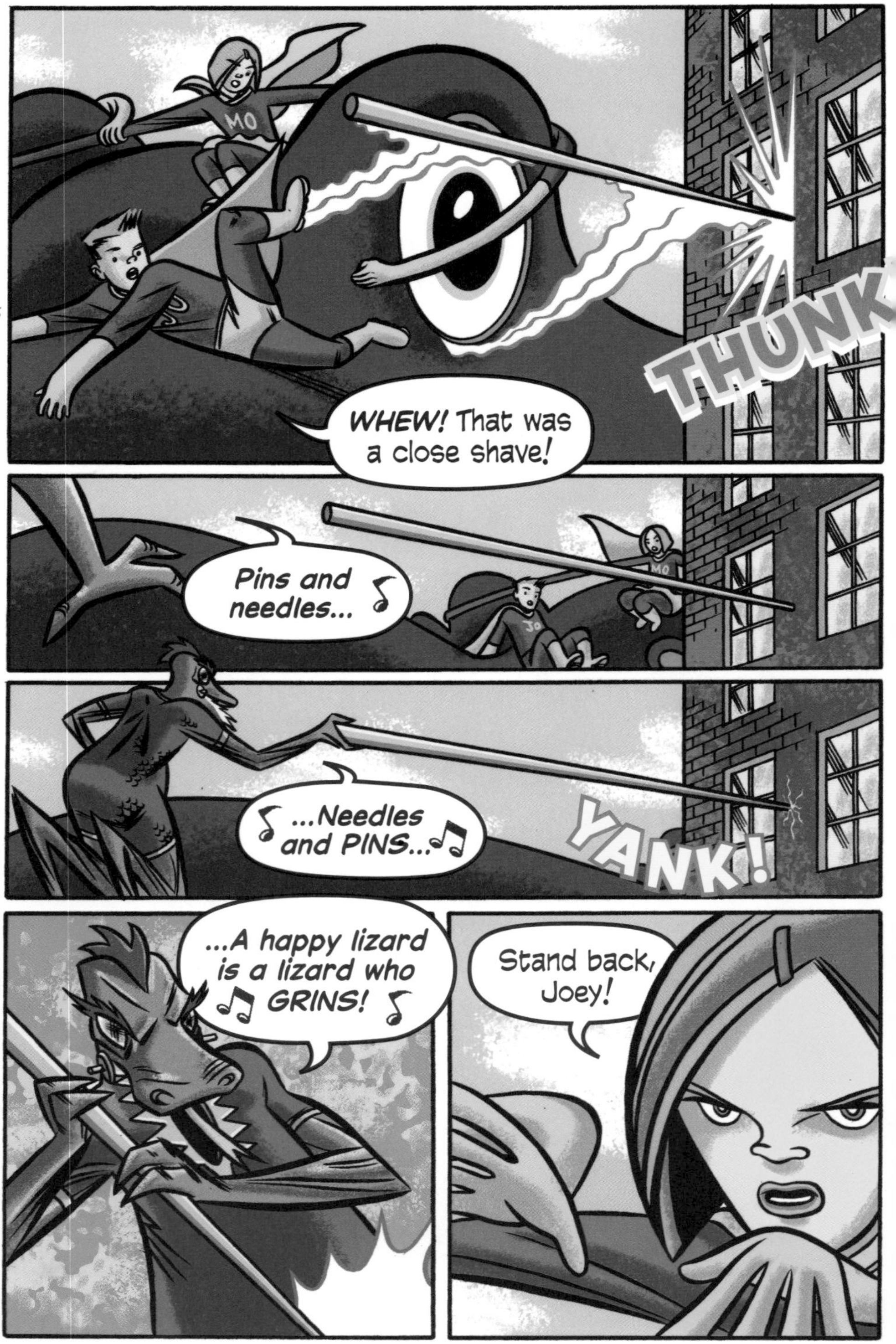
THUNK
WHEW! That was a close shave!
Pins and needles...
...Needles and PINS...
YANK!
...A happy lizard is a lizard who GRINS!
Stand back, Joey!

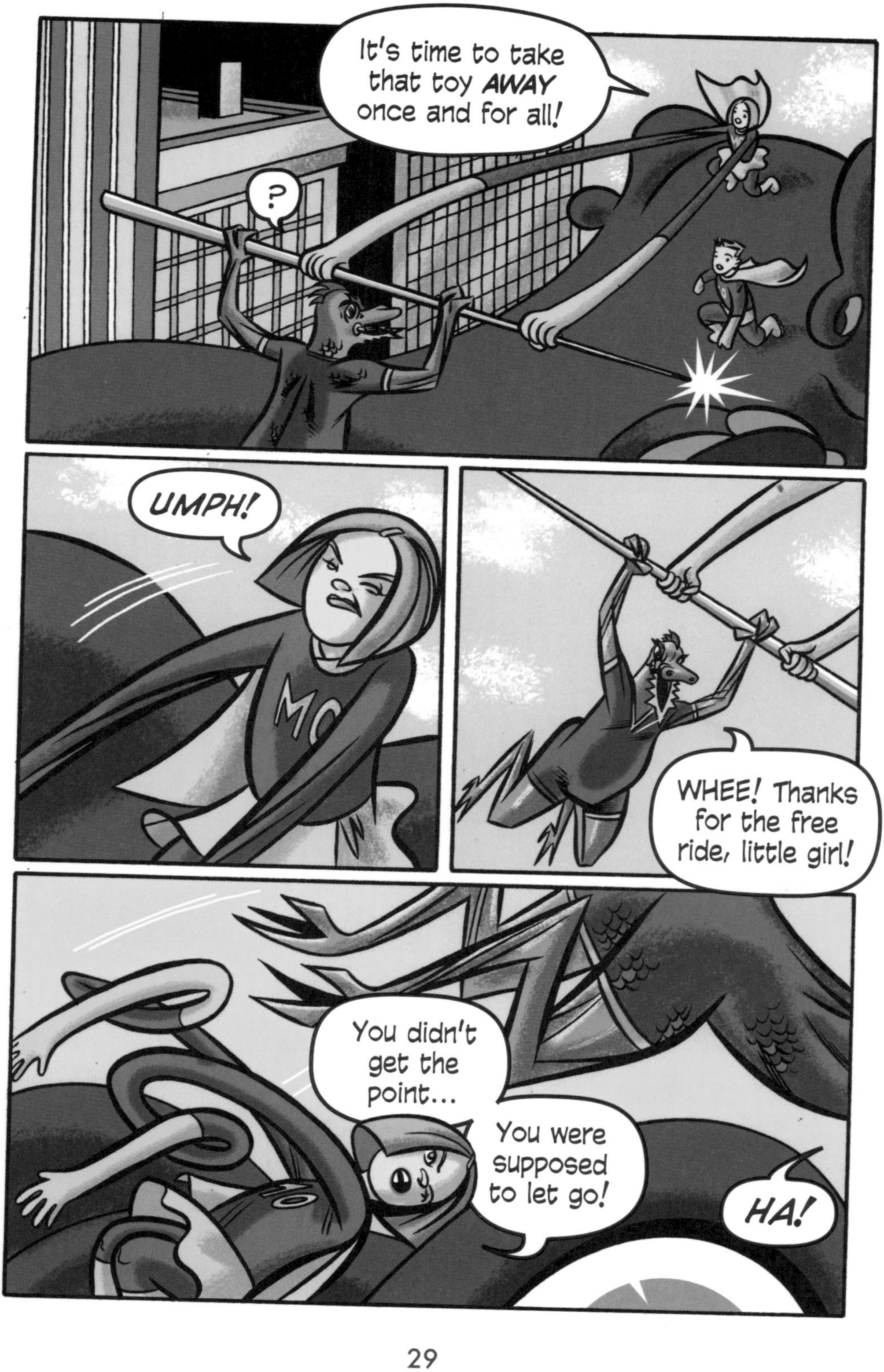
It's time to take that toy **AWAY** once and for all!
?
UMPH!
WHEE! Thanks for the free ride, little girl!
You didn't get the point...
You were supposed to let go!
HA!

CHAPTER THREE:

FIGHTING TOGETHER FOREVER...

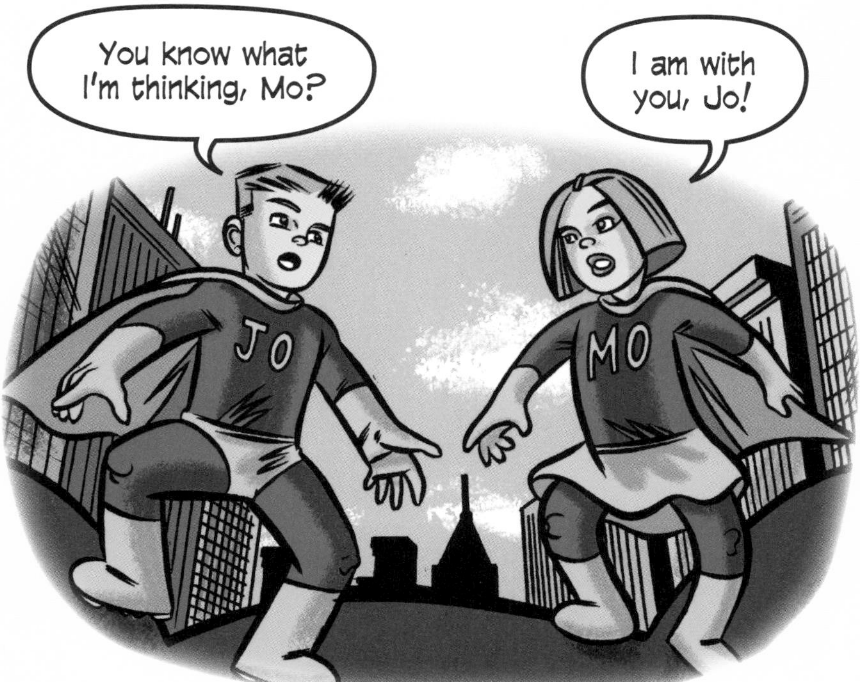
You know what I'm thinking, Mo?
I am with you, Jo!
JO
MO

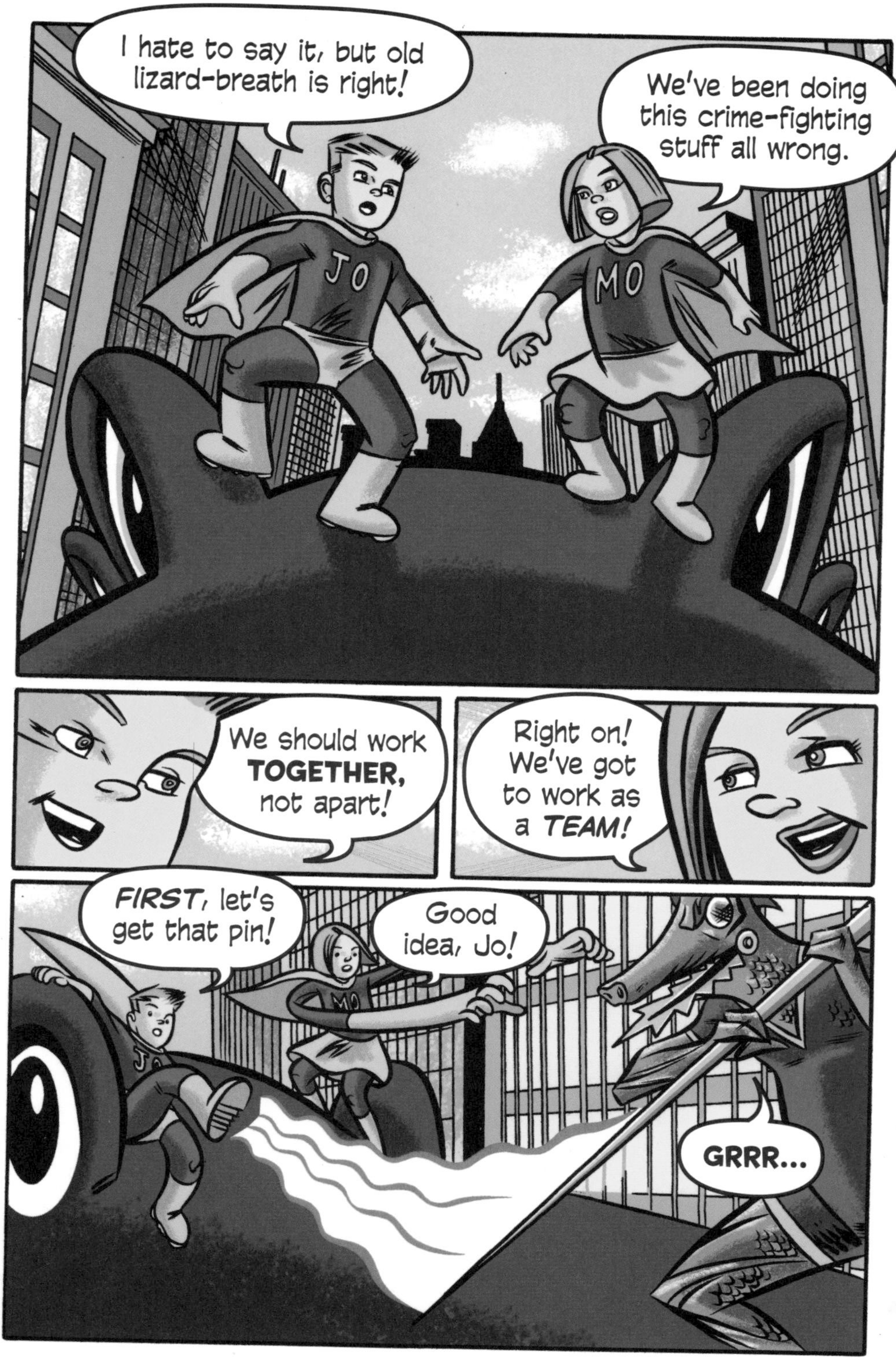
I hate to say it, but old lizard-breath is right!
We've been doing this crime-fighting stuff all wrong.
JO
MO
We should work **TOGETHER,** not apart!
Right on! We've got to work as a ***TEAM!***
FIRST, let's get that pin!
Good idea, Jo!
GRRR...

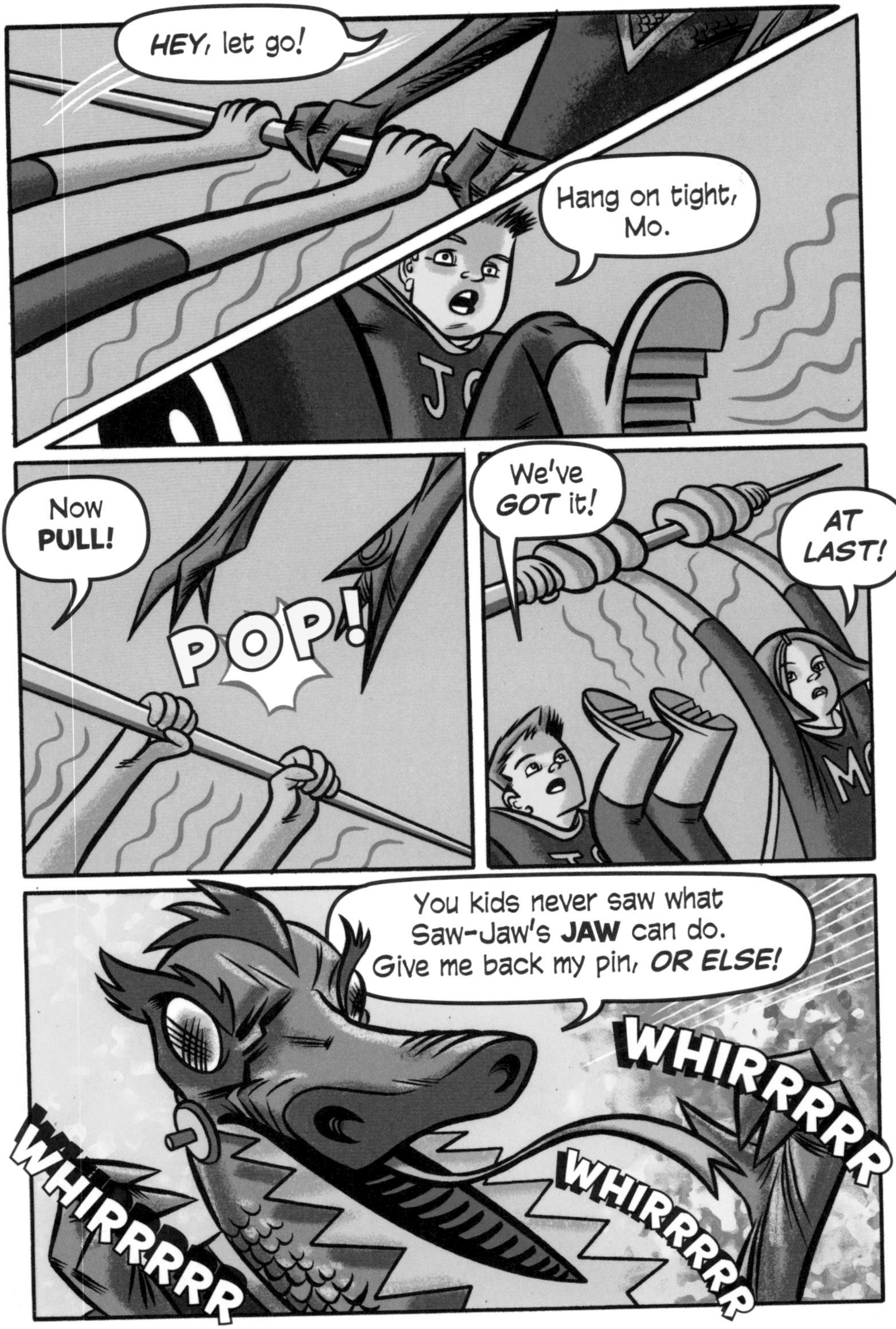
HEY, let go!
Hang on tight, Mo.
Now PULL!
POP!
We've GOT it!
AT LAST!
You kids never saw what Saw-Jaw's JAW can do. Give me back my pin, OR ELSE!
WHIRRRRRR
WHIRRRRRR
WHIRRRRRR

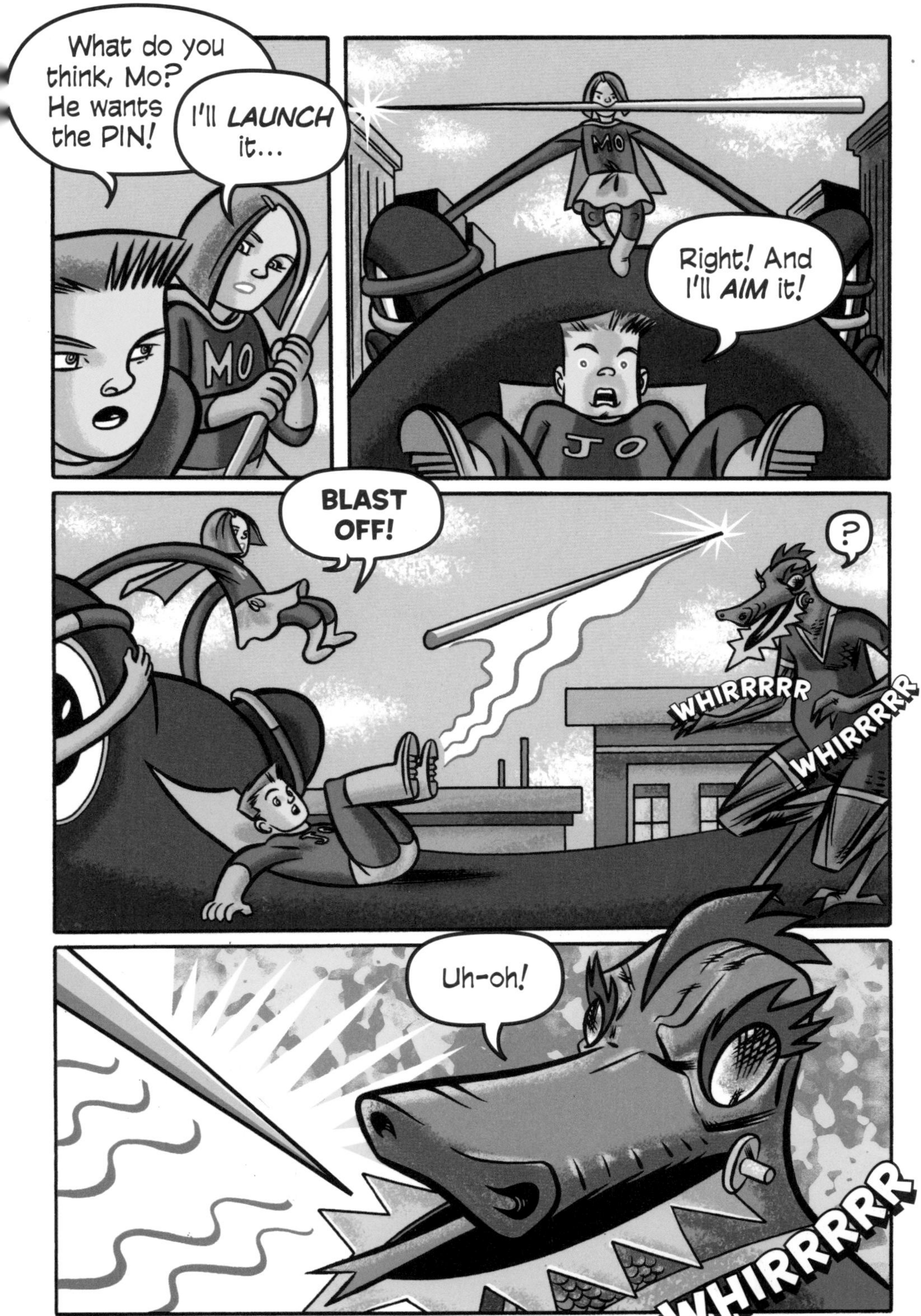
What do you think, Mo? He wants the PIN!
I'll LAUNCH it...
Right! And I'll AIM it!
BLAST OFF!
?
WHIRRRRR
WHIRRRRR
Uh-oh!
WHIRRRRR

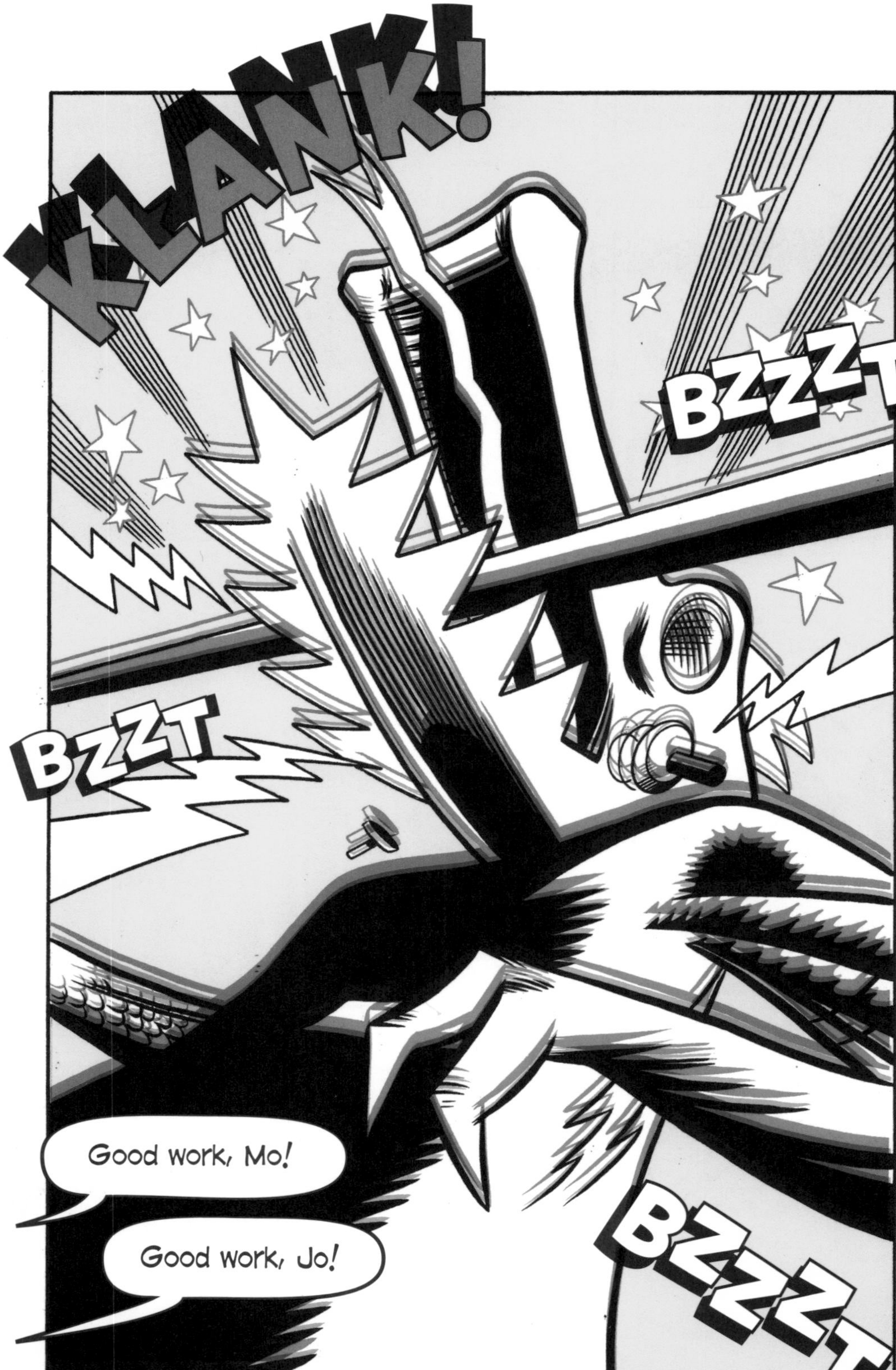
KLANK!
BZZZT
BZZT
Good work, Mo!
Good work, Jo!
BZZZT

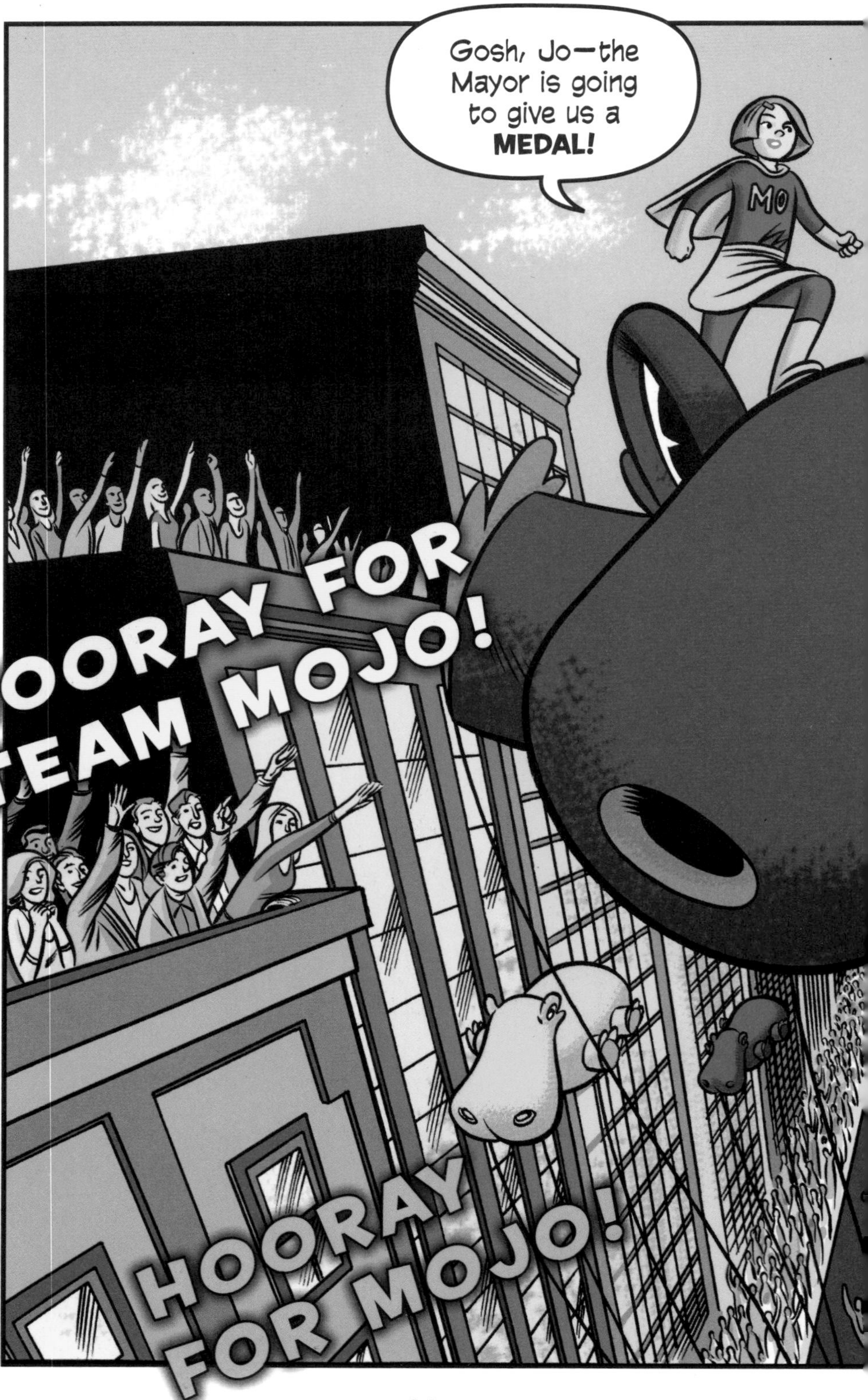
Gosh, Jo—the Mayor is going to give us a **MEDAL!**
HOORAY FOR TEAM MOJO!
HOORAY FOR MOJO!

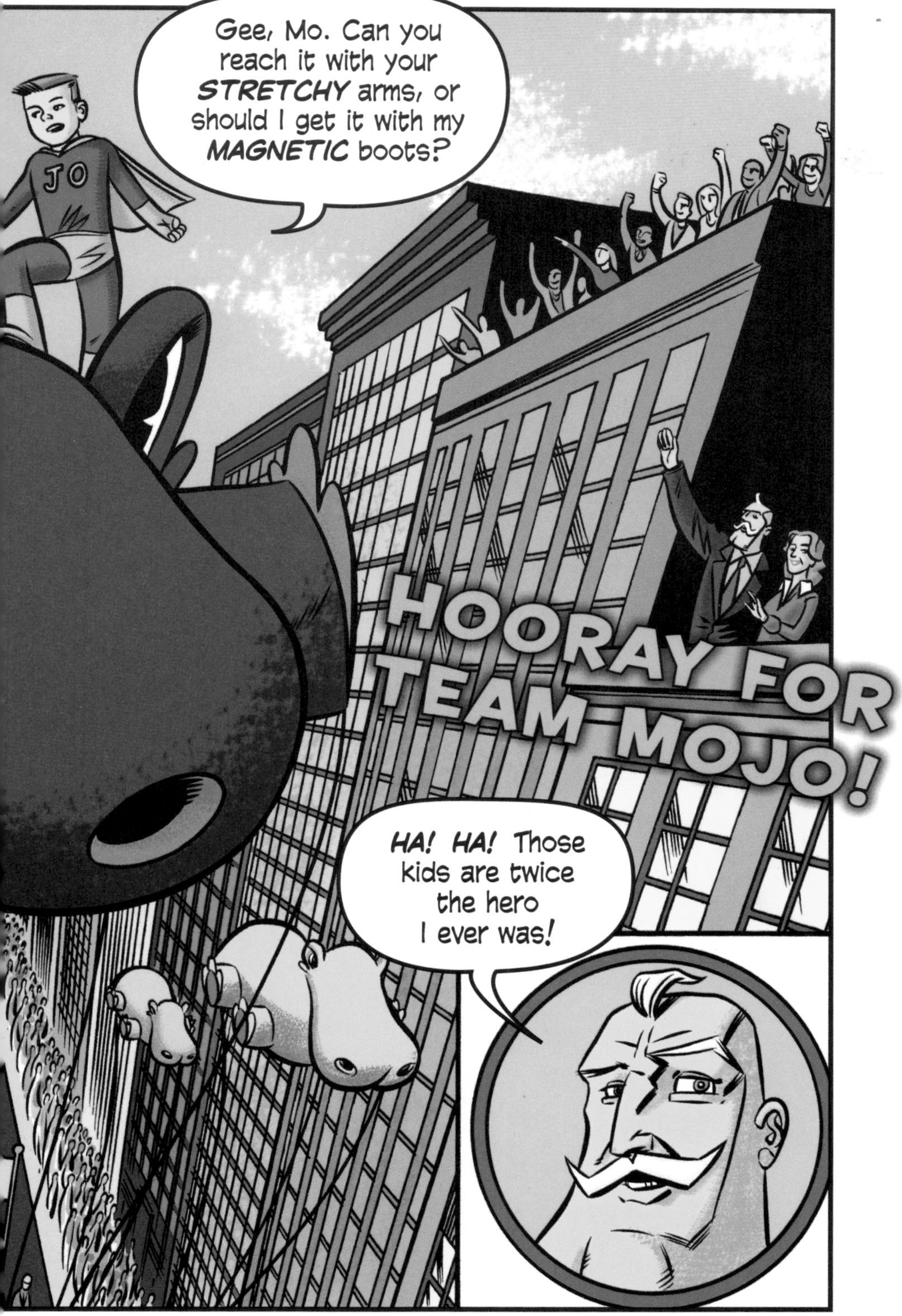
Gee, Mo. Can you reach it with your STRETCHY arms, or should I get it with my MAGNETIC boots?
HOORAY FOR TEAM MOJO!
HA! HA! Those kids are twice the hero I ever was!

THE END

ABOUT THE AUTHORS

JAY LYNCH, who wrote Mo and Jo's story, loved to read funny superhero comics like *Plastic Man* when he was a kid. When he wasn't reading comic books, he would draw his own cartoon characters on the sidewalk in front of his house—then hide in the bushes to hear what other kids had to say about his drawings! Jay grew up to become a legendary cartoonist and has helped create many popular humor products, including *Wacky Packages* and *Garbage Pail Kids*. If he could have any superpower, he'd like to know what color something is just by touching it.

DEAN HASPIEL, who drew Mo and Jo, used to read *Fantastic Four* and *Shazam!* when he was a kid. He admits that he used to fight with his brother all the time, too: "All siblings have a healthy rivalry, and so did we." Dean has illustrated Pulitzer Prize-winning author Michael Chabon's *The Escapist* and drawn superheroes for Marvel and DC Comics. He has created his own comic character, *Billy Dogma*, and is the founder of the webcomic collective ACT-I-VATE. If he could have any superpower, he'd like to fly, "because that would just be cool!"

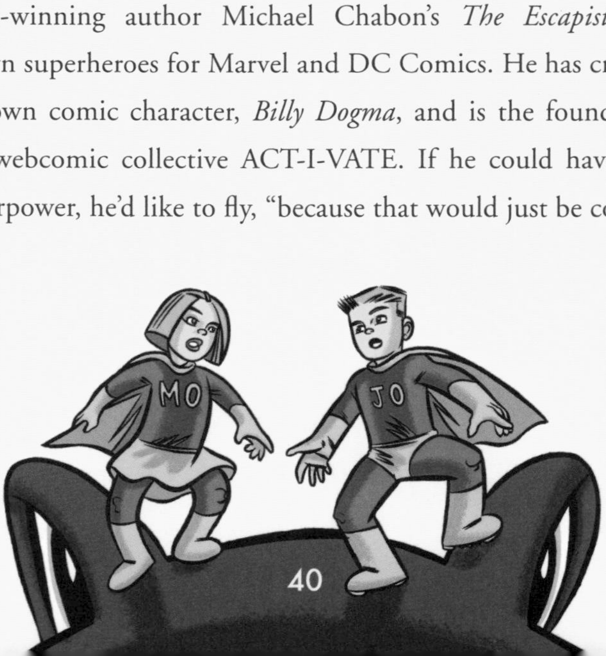
MO
JO